A Fedora Offense

Donna Kelly

Annie's®

AnniesFiction.com

Books in the Antique Shop Mysteries series

Library of Congress-in-Publication Data
A Fedora Offense / by Donna Kelly
p. cm.
I. Title
                    2017941229

AnniesFiction.com
(800) 282-6643
Antique Shop Mysteries™
Series Creator: Shari Lohner
Series Editor: Elizabeth Morrissey
Cover Illustrator: Bonnie Leick

10 11 12 13 14 | Printed in China | 9 8 7 6 5

1

"Sold to bidder 120." The auctioneer hammered his gavel and gestured toward a tall man whose eyes were hidden beneath a jet-black fedora.

Maggie Watson twisted her auction list between her hands and groaned. "That's the fourth time he's outbid me on a perfect piece for the shop."

"You both have a great eye for quality." June McGillis, the manager of Carriage House Antiques, followed Maggie's gaze across the packed ballroom at Twisdem Mansion. "Don't worry. We still have a few hours' worth of valuable antiques to see. We'll take home plenty of treasures."

"Thanks for the pep talk," Maggie said, watching the auctioneer amble over to the clerk who was tracking bids. "I learned everything I know from you."

"Psh, you're a natural." June waved away the compliment.

Maggie smiled. "We make a great team."

Maggie wasn't kidding. June had been a godsend when Maggie inherited her antiques shop and the adjacent home, Sedgwick Manor, after her aunt Evelyn died. Maggie had always admired antiques and old houses, but the notion of living in a manor house and running an antiques shop herself had never crossed her mind . . . until she had arrived in Somerset Harbor for the first time since childhood. She was pleasantly surprised to find that she felt at home among new friends. Soon after, she sold her cottage in Vermont and moved with Snickers, her trusty cat, to the small seacoast town in Maine.

A man who had been working the auction ran up and whispered something in the auctioneer's ear. "Excuse me," said the auctioneer, addressing the large crowd seated in the elegant ballroom of one of the town's oldest, largest, and most well-known houses. "We're taking a thirty-minute break to iron out a few things. Feel free to browse the first floor at your leisure."

Joining the line to leave the ballroom, Maggie took in the elegant features around her. She could easily picture women in long dresses and white-wigged men gliding across the gleaming hardwood floors two centuries ago. Her eyes drifted up one of the columns and gazed at the ornate scroll and leaves at the top. The room was certainly grand, with its gold-leaf details, massive marble fireplace, and elegant crystal chandeliers casting light from each end of the room.

She leaned closer to June. "Why do you suppose they're selling so many family heirlooms?"

June shuffled forward as the corpulent man in front of her moved ahead. "Nobody knows for sure. I've heard a bunch of rumors, which is nothing new for the Twisdem family. They've been gossip fodder for two hundred years. The good news for us is that the family's strange history will create a demand for the antiques."

"True, if we ever get our hands on any." Maggie searched the room for other dealers she knew, but she didn't see any others from the Somerset Harbor area. "This place is packed. I'm surprised we're the only local vendors."

"Seems strange that they only advertised it in larger cities," June said. "I would never have heard about it if my friend in Portland hadn't called to ask what I know about the Twisdems. We were lucky to get seats."

When they reached the door to the hall, Maggie looked at the mansion's floor plan in the auction program. "If we go left we can check out the salon." She sighed. "I wish we could see the second floor."

Stepping into the long, high-ceilinged hall, Maggie and June followed a long runner of deep green, crimson, and blue hues leading to the oval salon. They passed an array of narrow sofas, dark wood chairs, and occasional tables. China cabinets displayed glass pipe stands, Victorian figurines, and Wedgwood china.

Maggie stopped in the doorway of the salon and took in its curved pale yellow walls, ornate fireplace, and what appeared to be original furniture from the late 1700s, the love seats and chairs reupholstered in pale yellow, light blue, and gray.

"What a gorgeous room." Maggie drifted over to a portrait hanging above the fireplace and was caught by the lifelike countenances staring down at her: a father, a mother holding a swaddled infant, and a teenage daughter, all dressed in Victorian attire. It seemed to show the personality of each family member—the man properly stern, the woman defying the trend of the day with amused upturned lips, the daughter mischievous with twinkling eyes, and the infant sleeping peacefully.

Maggie's eyes burned with unexpected tears. *Why didn't we do a formal family portrait before Richard died?* When her daughter, Emily, was about the age of the girl in the photo, her husband had passed away unexpectedly, leaving Maggie to raise Emily alone. Now Emily was enrolled at St. Joseph's College in Vermont, and Maggie was learning the antiques business in Maine. *It's strange how life can turn on a dime.*

Maggie took a tissue from her purse and dabbed her eyes. June touched her arm. "You okay?"

"I'm fine," Maggie said, returning the tissue to her purse. "I was admiring the family portrait."

"It's well done. I hope it's not on the auction block," June said. "Family portraits should remain in the family."

"I agree."

A group of about twenty people entered the salon, causing everyone to squish together. Maggie nodded toward the window to the left of the fireplace. "There's our bidding opponent lurking in the crowd. I'm tempted to go over there and ask him to get into a bidding war with someone else."

"Somehow I doubt he'll back off just because you asked." June put a hand on Maggie's arm and led her across the room and into the salon doorway. "I don't recognize him, do you?"

"Nope. I wonder why he's dressed in solid black like a cat burglar. Seems a little dramatic for an estate auction." Maggie resisted the urge to get one more look at the mysterious man. "While we still have some time, let's check out the dining room."

Back in the hall, Maggie and June made their way to the dining room. Once inside, they admired the impressive thirteen-piece walnut Renaissance Revival dining set, fireplace, and two quaint sitting areas in arched alcoves. Maggie sighed appreciatively as she took in the room's decadent grandeur.

A few minutes later, Maggie and June returned to the ballroom and took their seats as the remainder of the crowd filtered in. Maggie ran her finger down the auction list, pausing on the first of four entries she'd starred as the most desirable. "This is the one I want the most," she said, gazing at a tiger maple sideboard with a set of three small drawers atop a larger drawer over a cabinet. "What a gorgeous piece."

"It is." June nodded. "I also like the oak bureau with the floral inlay."

Before they could discuss it further, the auctioneer grabbed his microphone and stepped to the head of the room. "I apologize for the delay. Now that we have solved our technical difficulties, the auction will continue."

The auctioneer was mesmerizing as he called the bidding. Over the last few years, Maggie had become better at following the quick pace. She watched Fedora Man handily outbid competitors for several pieces before the tiger maple sideboard was put on the auction block. As the bidding opened, she sat up straight and took one last look at Fedora Man before focusing on the auctioneer. Bidding for the sideboard started at $300. Maggie held up her bidding card first. She was joined by Fedora Man, and two other bidders seated behind her.

At $500, two bidders dropped out, leaving Maggie and Fedora Man.

Maggie raised her bidding paddle.

The auctioneer pointed to her and shouted, "$550!"

Fedora Man lifted his paddle.

"$600. Do I have $650?"

Maggie's breath quickened. "$650," she murmured, lifting her paddle. She braced for Fedora Man's response.

But she heard a cell phone ring instead. Fedora Man paused to peer at his phone, glared at Maggie, and held the phone to his ear. A moment later, he dashed out of the ballroom.

"Sold to bidder 351."

"Yes!" Maggie bounced in her seat.

June grinned at her. "I do believe I've created a monster. Your eyes are sparkling."

"Perhaps." Maggie held up her number. "Now I'm ready to bid on the cherrywood Queen Anne desk."

By the time Maggie and June finished delivery arrangements and shrugged into their coats, the sun had disappeared behind clouds and snow flurries drifted from the sky. They passed a line of cars and trudged down the winding drive toward Maggie's Volkswagen Jetta. When they reached it, Maggie unlocked the doors and turned to gaze at the formidable federal-style mansion.

"It looks sad, doesn't it?" She shivered and pulled her coat collar closer to her ears. "The house is well maintained, huge, and gorgeous, but—"

"Forlorn," June finished, opening the passenger-side door and sliding into the Jetta's leather seat.

"Exactly." Maggie eased behind the steering wheel. "Let's stop by The Busy Bean for lunch. Bidding wars always make me hungry."

. . . .

Maggie's fatigue and the wintry chill faded as soon as she and June entered The Busy Bean. Warm, cozy, and cheerful, the café's atmosphere was a colorful contrast to the overwhelming expanse and formality of the Twisdem Mansion. Outside was cold and gray, but the coffee shop was bathed in summery turquoise and lemon yellow.

"Hallelujah, you're finally here." Daisy Carter, The Busy Bean's Georgia-born owner, turned "here" into a two-syllable word. "We've been dying to know about the goings-on at the Twisdem Mansion. It's all everyone has talked about all day."

"The mansion is quite a place." Maggie shrugged out of her coat and draped it on the coatrack by the door. "The beautiful antiques and artwork are almost overwhelming."

June chuckled. "You should have seen Maggie battling Fedora Man. She was ferocious."

"Fedora Man?" Daisy raised an eyebrow. "That's a story I want to hear. James is at your favorite table. I'll be over to take your order and get my recap shortly."

As Daisy stepped over to grab a coffeepot from the warmer, Maggie looked toward the window, where a smiling James Bennett motioned to them. A town alderman and a regular at the coffee shop, James was one of the first people Maggie had met when she arrived in Somerset Harbor. He'd welcomed Maggie to the close-knit town and introduced her to many of the people she now considered good friends.

"Won't you ladies join me?" James placed his fork next to the pie slice on the plate in front of him, rose to his feet, and presented the chairs across from him with a flourish of his arm.

"Absolutely." Maggie hung her shoulder bag on the back of the chair opposite James and sat down while June took the chair next to her. "I'm so hungry I could eat a horse."

"Sorry, we're fresh out of horse." Daisy appeared at the end of the table, coffeepot in one hand and two cups in the other. "But I have killer sandwiches, your favorite soup, and mocha blend."

"No horse? I'm so disappointed." Maggie couldn't contain her smile. "I'm ready for a club sandwich and cup of split pea soup. And mocha blend."

"Ditto," June said. "Sounds good to me."

"I love women who know what they want," James said with a laugh.

Daisy poured their coffee and placed the pot on the table. She pulled her pad and pen from her pocket and jotted down their orders. "Don't tell the good stuff until I get back."

James arched an eyebrow as Daisy scurried back to the kitchen. "The good stuff?"

"June and I spent the morning at the Twisdem Mansion buying furniture for the shop. Daisy wants details."

"Understandable. Daisy has a keen interest in everything around here." James speared a forkful of apple pie. "How was the auction?"

Maggie and June took turns describing the crowd, the pieces of Twisdem family history for sale, and the purchases they'd made for Carriage House Antiques. The conversation paused momentarily when Daisy slid two orders of steaming soup and sandwiches on the table, but resumed as she scampered away to help other customers. When the crowd in the coffee shop thinned, Daisy returned, placed their checks on the table, and sat next to James as Maggie and June described the battle with the man in the fedora.

"Maggie was brilliant," June said.

Maggie took a sip of coffee. "He kept outbidding me until his cell phone rang, then he bolted from the room and never returned."

"I wonder what that was about," June said.

"He was certainly strange." Maggie shifted her gaze between James and Daisy. "What's the Twisdem story? Why are they selling their heirlooms? If anyone knows, it's got to be one of you two."

Daisy rubbed her hands together. "I've heard all kinds of rumors. There are dead bodies buried on the property. Or the family business was run into the ground by the younger generation. And my personal favorite—the original Twisdems were exiled royalty and now the family's returning to the ancestral palace."

James placed his fork on the now-empty pie plate, pushed it aside, and leaned forward. "It's a sad history, I'm afraid. The family's founding father, Samuel Twisdem, was a financial wizard who made his fortune in shipping toward the end of the 1700s. Later, the family diversified into insurance too. The family home remained here while the business offices were in Portland and Boston."

"Sounds like quite the success story," Maggie said.

"The business became larger and more powerful until the late 1960s. Then members of the family were involved in a mysterious car crash in 1970. It's become somewhat of a local legend." James paused to take a sip of water. "The businesses still exist, but the family . . . well, if anyone named Twisdem is still around, they're the reclusive type."

Maggie shivered. "Mysterious car crash? Was the car tampered with?"

"No one really knows. The car was too badly damaged."

"Where did it happen?" Maggie's curiosity sizzled.

"They were heading toward Portland. From what I've heard, charred remnants of the car were found at the bottom of a deep ravine." James paused. "Remember, this happened slightly before my time."

Daisy turned in her chair and checked out the few customers left in the coffee shop to make sure she wasn't needed, then returned her attention to James. "So, why are they auctioning off family treasures now? That's what everybody wants to know."

"From what I heard from a friend in Portland, whoever owns the house is selling the contents and remodeling the mansion." He shrugged. "Evidently, they have more contemporary tastes, so they're cleaning house."

"What a sad story," June said. "It's like the personal history of the place is disappearing."

Tears welled in Maggie's eyes as she thought of how much her own family had changed over the years. First she'd lost her mother, her best friend and confidant. Then, Richard, her husband and the love of her life, suffered a fatal aortic aneurysm. Most recently, she'd lost Evelyn, her beloved aunt and mentor. But she still had Emily, of course, and her father. Guilt washed over her at the thought of her dad. When was the last time she had called him? She couldn't remember.

"Maggie?" James's voice interrupted her thoughts. "Are you all right?"

She dabbed her eyes with a napkin and cleared her throat. "Yes, of course." She pulled her auction list from her purse and jotted down a note: *Call Dad.* Standing up, Maggie swept the check off the table. "I'd best be getting home. Thank you for sharing the Twisdem story."

"My pleasure," James said, smiling.

Daisy led Maggie and June to the register and rang up their purchases. "Are you really okay, Maggie?"

"I'm a bit tired." Maggie waved away the bills and change in Daisy's outstretched hand. "That's your tip."

"Ready, Maggie?" June asked.

Maggie nodded and stepped toward the door. As she reached for the handle, the door opened and a tall man entered, his arm brushing against her shoulder. "Excuse m—" Maggie's voice froze when she looked up and found herself face-to-face with Fedora Man.

2

His face stormy, the mysterious man curtly nodded his fedora-topped head and ducked around her into the café. Maggie frowned the whole way back to Carriage House Antiques.

"Are you coming in?" June put her hand on the car door handle.

"I'm too curious about the Twisdems to concentrate on business." Maggie drummed her fingertips on the steering wheel. "It'd be fun to have some additional back story about the family to go with the pieces we bought. I think I'll nose around the newspaper morgue a bit. Thanks for going to the auction with me."

"I enjoyed it. Seeing the inside of the famed Twisdem Mansion was worth taking the time and fighting the crowd." June opened the car door. "I doubt you'll miss much at the shop this afternoon. Have fun at the newspaper."

"I will. Hopefully I'll learn something too."

Maggie watched June cross the parking lot and unlock the door to the antiques shop. She couldn't shake the foreboding feeling she'd had since Fedora Man bumped into her as she left The Busy Bean. He hadn't said a word, but the look on his face had given her chills. Any inkling she'd had to grill him about why he had kept outbidding her vanished when she had seen his grim expression. He was older than she'd imagined, maybe in his sixties, his face weathered. Had the brief contact been deliberate? Was he in a hurry to meet someone or simply not paying attention?

Maggie glanced down as she put the car in gear and saw the wrinkled auction list sticking out of the top of her bag. Her rounded cursive handwriting caught her attention. "'Call Dad,'" she read aloud.

Oh Dad, why did you have to move so far away after Mom died? But Maggie knew why. He'd wanted to return to Michigan, where he grew up, to live near his sister and two brothers, an aunt and uncles Maggie barely knew. Richard and Emily had been the center of her life. Had Dad left because she'd been too preoccupied with her own family to be more involved with his life?

As she glanced in the rearview mirror, Maggie's cell phone chime pierced her thoughts. She put the car back in park and answered the phone. "Hello?"

"Maggie, this is your father." Neil Segal's voice was deeper than she remembered.

"Dad!" A mixture of happiness and concern filled Maggie. "I was just thinking of you. How are you?"

"I'm fine. Keeping busy. You have been on my mind." His words were breathless.

Maggie reached for the auction list and played with the bottom corners, folding and unfolding them as she searched for words. "How are Aunt Rebekah, Uncle Carl, and Uncle Joe?"

"They're fine. We're all feeling the cold a little more these days." He took deep breaths between his words. "Maggie . . ."

"Yes, Dad?"

"Maggie, I'm sorry, I need to go. I love you. Good-bye."

"I love you too, Dad," Maggie said, puzzled.

But he was already gone.

"That was strange." She toyed with the idea of calling him back, but he'd sounded distracted. Maybe this wasn't a good time to talk. She'd try again later.

As Maggie pulled out of her parking spot, she realized that she frankly didn't know her father's side of the family any better than she knew the Twisdem family. *Well, at least I can find out more about the Twisdems today.*

. . . .

Armed with a notebook, a pen, and a hand warmer packet in each coat pocket, Maggie pushed open the door to the white clapboard building that housed the *Somerset Harbor Herald*. She had visited the paper often enough to grow accustomed to the newsroom's pungent smell of printer's ink, finding that it added to the place's old-time atmosphere. Past the rack of newspapers and behind the glass-topped wooden counter, Thaddeus Jablonsky, the editor, sat at one of two oak desks, tapping on a computer keyboard.

"Good afternoon, Thad." Maggie leaned on the counter and waved her pad at the empty desk. "Running the office solo today?"

He looked over the reading glasses sitting low on his nose. "Not for long. I sent Adrian to the Twisdem place to see what's happening over there. Heard through the grapevine that it's quite an auction, but the auctioneer wasn't allowing the press in. We haven't been able to get through to the family, despite Adrian camping out on the grounds."

"June and I were there earlier today. Wall-to-wall people, lots of bidding, and rumors flying." Maggie slid her notebook on the counter. "That's why I'm here, actually. We bought pieces at the auction and it spurred my interest in the family history. I figured Carriage House customers would be curious about it too."

"And you want to search the archives," he finished for her. "How far back do you want to go?"

"To the crash."

"Ah, the legendary accident that nearly wiped out a major corporation. I was a kid in 1970, so I don't remember much about it. And I'm embarrassed to say that I know nothing about the modern-day Twisdems either, despite being an ace reporter." Thad rubbed his hand over the top of his thinning brown hair. "You're welcome to search the archives. I imagine a story like that would have been on the front page. Let me know if you find anything interesting."

"Will do." Maggie opened the door to the stairway, flipped the light switch, and headed up the steps. At the top of the stairs, Maggie crossed a small hallway and entered what had once been the living room of a small apartment. It now served as the *Herald*'s morgue, where back issues of the newspaper were stored the old-fashioned way, inside white boxes stacked on metal racks. Opening each box was like entering a time machine. Today, she was traveling, so to speak, to the dawn of the 1970s. She'd become a frequent visitor to the *Herald* morgue since moving to Somerset Harbor, having adopted Aunt Evelyn's habit of researching antiques purchased for the shop and recording her findings in a journal. She had a pretty good idea of where to start looking for issues from the right era.

Shivering in the unheated room, Maggie tore open the two foil packets in her pockets, removed the palm-size hand warmers, and held one in each hand while scanning the shelves on the middle section of the sixth row of racks. When she found boxes with *1970* on them, she returned the hand warmers to her pockets and lugged the boxes to the table in the back corner of the room. No one had mentioned when the accident occurred, so she began with the box labeled *January 1970*.

The front page of each issue held something she found amusing. Among other things, she came across a photo of a young Ruth Harper with her blue ribbon-winning quilt at the Winter Warming Festival, an article featuring a younger Ina Linton in a quest to save a historical building, and an update on the restoration of Old Faith Chapel.

Maggie caught her breath as she turned to the January 19 issue. She found the bold headline, *Twisdems Dead in Fiery Crash: Daughter on Life Support*, stretched across the front page. Her eyes widened when she focused on the photo below it. Blackened, twisted remnants of what was, according to the cutline, the family's 1969 Cadillac were sprinkled at the bottom of a ravine along Old Mills Landing Road.

A shiver ran down her spine. *How terrifying that must have been for them.*

She pulled her notebook and pen closer and scribbled notes as she read: *Old Mills Landing Road, wet roads, one-car crash, parents Andrew and Lucille Twisdem and son Scott Andrew Twisdem dead; daughter Marilyn Ann Twisdem on life support, not expected to recover.*

The article included a brief family history dating back to the 1700s, mostly about patriarch Samuel Twisdem, a shipping magnate and one of the founders of Somerset Harbor. The writer concluded the article by stating that the future of the family business was uncertain.

Chilled by the cold air and the details of the Twisdem tragedy, Maggie sat back in the chair, stuck her hands in the coat pockets, and wrapped her fingers around the warmer packets.

She released the hand warmer in her right pocket and flipped the newspaper pages until she came to the next issue, dated January 26. The main headline read, *Twisdem Heiress Remains on Life Support, Next of Kin Sought.*

In addition to recounting the various gifts the family had given to the community, the article included a plea from the Somerset Harbor Police Chief for Twisdem family relatives to contact the police department, a "no comment" statement from a representative of the Twisdem Corporation, and a few words from the mayor, Walt Waters: *"This branch of the Twisdem family is destined to end with Marilyn Twisdem, who will not survive removal from the ventilator according to a hospital employee. But the impact of this family on our community will be felt far into the future."*

"No kidding," Maggie muttered. She scanned the remaining newspapers from 1970 but found no further mention of Marilyn Twisdem.

Adding up everything she had read and heard, Maggie determined that the next of kin must have been tracked down and had kept up the mansion and run Twisdem Corporation since the crash.

Only vaguely satisfied with her research, Maggie returned the boxes to the shelf and descended the stairs to the newsroom. The old clock behind Thad's desk showed it was after five. She smiled and waved to the editor, who had a phone to his ear, and left the building.

· · · · · · · · · · · · · · · · ·

The following morning, Maggie was surprised to find June standing outside the door of Carriage House Antiques, one hand on her hip and the other scratching her head, staring at a large cardboard box resting on the stoop.

June gestured toward the box. "I don't know what to make of this."

"What is it?"

"I'm not sure. I was straightening up the shop when I heard a car in the driveway. By the time I walked to the front of the shop and peeked out the window, the parking lot was empty. I figured someone was just turning around in the drive, so I went back inside to work on the Valentine's Day display." June shivered and rubbed her hands along the upper sleeves of her bulky green sweater. "A few minutes later, I heard a sneeze from outside and ran to the door. When I looked outside, a man was rummaging through the box."

Maggie shivered too, but she was plenty warm in her coat. "Did he seem threatening?"

"He ran off before I opened the door. He must have heard me unlocking it and didn't want a confrontation. Did you see anyone walking down the road?"

Maggie shook her head. "I passed several cars, but nobody on foot." Noticing that June's nose was turning red, she added, "Let's get this box inside before you freeze."

June propped the shop door open with a decorative milk can. The box was surprisingly heavy, so they carried it together to the workroom in the back and placed it on the table. While June went to close the door, Maggie peered into the box and discovered a piece of paper wedged down the side. She wiggled it out and held it up to the light. *Please sell. Keep the money.*

"Take a look at this." Maggie handed the note to June as she entered the workroom.

June toyed with the cloisonné ballpoint pen hanging on a chain around her neck and examined the note. "No signature. That's odd. Anything of value?"

Maggie lifted out the box's contents. By the time she reached the bottom, she'd collected a man's wooden valet box, several pieces of sterling silver, and a stack of old vinyl records. "No high-ticket items, but look at these albums," Maggie said, flipping through the stack. "The Beatles, Otis Redding, The Doors, Steppenwolf, and Creedence Clearwater Revival. My dad would love these."

June chuckled. "I doubt we could sell them. Not much call for dinosaurs these days."

"I should bring it all up to the house and have a listen later." Maggie returned the records to the box.

"I think there's an old record player stashed in the back room somewhere. Your aunt never threw anything away."

"And I'm glad of it." Maggie picked up the note and read it again. "I wonder who dropped off the box."

June ran her hand over the valet box and shrugged. "It's not like we've never had someone donate before, but to have someone poking around in it right on the front porch? What was the man looking for?"

Maggie sighed. "I'm asking myself the same thing."

3

Maggie set the portable record player down by the side door next to the box of albums from the shop, then flexed her fingers to shake off the cold from the short drive between shop and home. She decided the records could wait for later. The best remedy for her chill would be herbal tea and reading in one of her favorite spots.

The old grandfather clock in the hallway finished striking twelve times as Maggie pushed open the sliding door and followed her tabby cat, Snickers, into the library. She laid the Portland daily newspaper and her tea on a tobacco stand, then switched on a Tiffany table lamp.

Maggie settled into a cozy reproduction Regency chair with well-worn leather cushions, and Snickers curled up in her lap. She picked up the mug of tea and read the words emblazoned on the side: *Any day spent stitching is a good day.* It had been a birthday gift from Emily. Maggie took a sip and tried to think of the last time she'd taken needle in hand for a stitching project.

After returning her cup to the coaster on the tobacco stand, Maggie unfolded the newspaper and skimmed the front section before turning to the Arts section. Her eyes stopped when they came to the headline *Legendary Rocker Cole Loveren to Appear in Portland.* She smiled. The musician had always been her dad's favorite. Neil had played his records when he came home from his long days as a bank manager. His cars were always stocked with cassettes, and later CDs, of every album Loveren released. Neil especially admired the artist's diversity. The superstar's music, although considered rock and roll, combined many genres, from blues and jazz to country and folk.

Maggie replayed in her mind her last conversation with her father. *Why did he hang up so quickly?* Fear shot through her. *Could he be seriously ill and keeping it from me?* She pulled out her cell phone and dialed his number, then frowned when she reached his voice mail. "Hi Dad, it's Maggie. Just thought I'd see if you were up for a chat. Give me a ring when you can. I love you."

She set her phone on the arm of the chair, then reached down to pet Snickers, who purred with gusto. "Well, I can't do much more about Dad's mysterious behavior, but I can dig for information about the Twisdems. Information about the furniture's former owners might entice buyers, especially if it's interesting."

James would be a great place to start. A restoration expert who specialized in older homes, he enjoyed discussing local history. Even if he didn't know much himself, he could certainly point her in the right direction of someone who did. Maybe they could meet for coffee now before she headed to the grocery store. The possibility made her smile. She dialed his number and waited to hear his voice.

"Hi, Maggie. How are you?"

"I'm filled with questions about the Twisdem family. May I buy you a cup of coffee and pick your brain for a little while?"

"I'd like nothing more, but I'm walking into a meeting as we speak. I'm afraid I'll be tied up most of the day." Did she imagine the disappointment in his voice? "I'll call you first thing in the morning. Will that work?"

"Sure. We'll talk tomorrow." She tried to hide her own disappointment. "Thanks."

Maggie ended the call and sighed. "Well, Snickers, maybe one of the ladies at the historical society meeting tonight will have information about the elusive Twisdems."

· · · · · · · · · · · · · · · · ·

The sun had long since sunk below the horizon when Maggie locked her car and walked up the sidewalk to the Victorian painted lady that housed the Somerset Harbor Historical Society. The bright teal and pale rose of the home's exterior was subdued in the moonlight and soft glow of streetlamps. She paused briefly to gaze at the moon, then hurried up the steps for the society's weekly meeting. Having spent the afternoon with June preparing the shop to take delivery of the items from Twisdem Mansion, Maggie was filled with excitement to learn more about the family. The ladies in the historical society were sure to have information.

Maggie walked through the grand old museum until she found her friends gathered around the large dining room table, which was laden with cups of coffee and plates of Daisy's chocolate fudge cake.

"Hi," Maggie said, passing under the rounded arch into the dining room.

"Oh good, you're here," Daisy said. "Everyone is waiting for an update about the Twisdem antiques. June wouldn't say anything until you got here."

Historical society president Ruth Harper was seated at the head of the table and patted the back of an empty chair next to her. "Sit here. Your cake is waiting for you. Unfortunately, Ina won't be joining us. She's still battling a sinus infection and is stuck at home per doctor's orders."

Maggie took the chair. "I'm not sure what's worse for her, the infection or being out of the loop." In her seventies, Ina was not only spry for her age, but she was also a walking, talking history book where Somerset Harbor was concerned.

Twirling a pen above a small notebook next to her plate, June said, "We're hoping all of you can help us pull together information and stories about the family to include with the antiques."

"I knew Scott Twisdem, God rest his soul," Ruth said. She cut a bite from her cake slice and dragged it through a line of frosting but returned it to the plate uneaten. "I didn't know him well, though. We ran in different circles. He was a trust-fund baby."

Maggie took a sip of coffee from a dainty cup with a vine of purple flowers encircling the lip. "What do you remember about him?"

"Good-looking with dark hair and eyes to match. Artistic. I heard he wanted to go to art school. That's about all I can tell you." Ruth scraped cake crumbs into a pile in the center of her almost-empty plate. "The family was very good to the town and donated generous amounts to the hospital, church, and school, but most of their hobnobbing was done in Portland, I think."

Liz Young—whose husband, David, was the minister of Old Faith Chapel—bobbed her head. "The church is filled with plaques honoring the Twisdems for their service, but they haven't been active in the church since before David became pastor. I've never met any of the family members."

"I'm not much help, I'm afraid." Fran Vosburg toyed with the bottom of the dark ponytail hanging just past her shoulders. "To my knowledge, not a single Twisdem has darkened the doors of The Quilt Cupboard since I opened. I sure would love to see the inside of the mansion, though."

"Oh, why didn't I think of this before?" Ruth tapped herself on the forehead. "You should talk to my old friend Cynthia Moorman. Well, she was Cynthia Evers back then. She was Scott Twisdem's high school sweetheart. She broke up with him shortly before the accident, but I can't remember why. It was a long time ago."

"I'll do that. How can I reach her?" Maggie pulled a notepad and pen from her purse.

"She lives on Cliff Road. It's a yellow house with white shutters. I think the number is 304." Ruth's face softened. "I haven't seen Cynthia in far too long. I'll call her and tell her to expect a visit from you." Ruth seemed lost in thought for a minute, then shook her head as if pushing memories from her mind. "Well, enough of the Twisdem family," she said, handing a stack of papers to Maggie to pass around. "Let's read the minutes from the last meeting before the night gets away from us."

After the minutes were approved, the ladies posed ideas for upcoming fund-raisers and discussed the possibility of making a donation to the renovation of the school auditorium. As they chatted, Maggie's thoughts drifted to Scott Twisdem and the accident that claimed his life. *What I wouldn't give to find out what really happened to that poor family.*

· · · · · · · · · · · · · · · · ·

Driving home, Maggie's thoughts bounced from her father's odd phone call to the fateful crash that devastated the Twisdem family long ago. By the time she pulled into the manor's circular driveway, Maggie was itching to immerse herself in history. Scott Twisdem would have been about the same age as her father. Maybe learning about that time period would make her feel closer to both of them.

She brought the car to a stop in the curve of the driveway and admired the nineteenth-century Colonial Revival manor for a moment. Then, she adjusted the wool scarf around her neck, grabbed her purse, and slid out of the car. She hurried to the door, feeling the chill of the wind in her bones. When she opened it, Snickers greeted her with loud purrs while making figure eights around her legs.

Maggie bent down and scratched the cat behind his ears. She loved the sound of his purring. "It's nice to have a welcoming committee."

She crossed the foyer and meandered through the kitchen into the breakfast room with Snickers in her wake. Hanging her coat and scarf on the coatrack by the side door, Maggie's foot brushed against the two boxes she'd set there earlier. The record player was the larger of the two, and had its own built-in case complete with a handle that made it resemble a suitcase. Old vinyl records, both albums and singles, filled the smaller box.

"What do you say, Snickers, want to listen to some old-time rock and roll?" The cat twitched his ears and backed away. "Coward." Maggie laughed, then grasped the record player by the handle and carried it to the library, where she eased it down on a square table below the window. Then she returned to the kitchen, picked up the box of records, and carted that to the library too.

After opening the record player and plugging it in, she dug through the box of records. Buried under those she and June had seen the previous day, she discovered albums by Chicago Transit Authority, Bob Dylan, The Moody Blues, Simon and Garfunkel, and her dad's favorite, Cole Loveren.

Maggie flipped through the stack until she found her favorite Simon and Garfunkel album. She removed the record from its sleeve, placed it on the turntable, and chuckled as she readied the machine to play it. *What would Emily and her college friends think of this fossil of a music player?*

As the comforting sounds of Simon and Garfunkel filtered into the room, Maggie sank into her favorite chair, tilted her head back, and closed her eyes, allowing the music to wash over her. She sat with her mind happily empty except for the familiar tunes for nearly half an hour.

When the last song ended, she rubbed her eyes and opened them, then rose to flip the record. Maggie lifted the stylus, set it on its rest, and turned the record to the "B" side. She moved the stylus to the edge of the record once again. A split second before she placed the needle on the record, the sound of a knock on glass echoed across the library. Maggie dropped the stylus on the record, causing it to screech, and looked out the window.

A pair of eyes stared back at her.

She ran to the fireplace and grabbed the fire iron. Her heart pounded an unnatural rhythm in her tightened chest. Inching up to the window, she peered beyond the curtain. Illuminated by the streetlamp, snow flurries drifted from the sky. The trespasser had vanished into the otherwise calm night. Had she imagined the eyes at the window?

Maggie startled when she felt a brush against her legs. She scooped Snickers up and nuzzled his fur. "I think it's time we go to bed."

With Snickers nestled in her arms, Maggie turned on small lights in several rooms and double-checked that all exterior doors were locked. After testing the door to the terrace, she stopped to pull a small pink canister from a drawer in the kitchen. She headed to her bedroom, a cat in one hand and pepper spray in the other.

4

"You didn't call the police?" June's eyes widened. "Whyever not?"

Maggie kept her eyes focused on the Valentine's Day table-for-two display they were setting up. She shrugged as she smoothed a dainty doily in the center of the small round table. "And tell them what? That I thought I saw a face at my library window, but I wasn't sure? The snow flurries would have covered any tracks he'd made, assuming it was a man. All I saw was a set of eyes, if I saw anything at all."

"At least they would have had an official report in case anything else happens." June deftly rolled a pink cloth square, slipped a silver napkin ring around it, and placed it across the table from a matching one. "You know something else will happen. It always does. Evelyn roused her share of mischief while researching antiques, but I believe you're even better at unearthing trouble than she was."

"Who, me?" Maggie said, fluttering her eyelids and resting the fingers of one hand just below the neckline of her pale blue sweater. "Do I look like a troublemaker?"

"Sweetie, you look like an angel, but for some reason you tend to attract people who are the exact opposite." June placed a pair of slender ornate candlesticks in the center of the doily. "Do you think these are too fancy? They were wedged in between the records and the side of the box I found outside yesterday. Makes me think the box came from someone wealthy, since we don't usually get silver-plated hand-me-downs."

"They're perfect." Maggie nabbed a small Lenox bowl from a nearby oak sideboard and placed it between the candlesticks.

"Wouldn't a few flowers look great floating in this bowl? It shouldn't cost too much to replace them a couple of times during the month. I'm going to see Cynthia Moorman this afternoon. I'll pick some up on the way back."

"That will be perfect." June stood with her hands on her hips and looked at the result of the morning's work with a critical eye.

Maggie checked her watch. It was nearing twelve thirty. "I'd best freshen up a bit and get going. I want to have plenty of time to visit with Cynthia."

June pushed the candlesticks an inch closer to each other. "Happy sleuthing!"

Maggie put on her coat and braced herself for the whipping wind on the short trek to the house. She was halfway across the path when she heard her cell phone ring in her coat pocket. She hoped James was calling to set up that coffee date. Pausing to fish it out, she gave a start when she saw the number on the screen. It wasn't James.

Taking a deep breath, she switched on the phone. "Hi, Dad. How are you?"

"I'm fine." *He doesn't sound fine. He sounds weird.* "How are things there?"

She shivered as the wind rendered her coat almost useless. "Windy at the moment." Maggie fought the urge to ask if everything was okay. After all, he wasn't a child. "I read in the paper that Cole Loveren will be appearing in Portland. It made me remember how much you played his music when I was a kid and we danced to it in the living room."

"We sure did a lot of dancing in the living room when you were little."

Maggie sighed. The conversation felt like a cat-and-mouse game. *Why won't he tell me what's wrong?* "Someone dropped off a box of vinyl records at the shop. Maybe I'll resurrect the living room dance tradition."

Her father coughed as the wind whistled again. "How about when I come for a visit in three days? It'll be fun."

Maggie froze. The wind had muffled his words, but she was sure he'd said he was arriving in just a few days.

Scrambling to gather her thoughts, Maggie stepped onto her porch and put the key in the door as apprehension washed over her. This seemed like good news, but why so little notice? It wasn't like him. He always planned everything far in advance. "That's great, Dad. I'll have the guest room ready."

"Sounds good, Mags. The plane lands in Portland at eight that night. I'll get a rental car so you don't need to drive to the airport. Should be at your place by ten."

Questions spun in Maggie's head as she stepped into the breakfast room. Holding the phone under her chin, she shook off her coat and hung it on the coatrack. "But what about—"

"I have to go, Maggie. Lots to do. I'll see you soon." With a click, he was gone again.

Maggie bent down and scratched Snickers behind his ears. "Dad's acting strange."

After giving the cat a bit of attention and a couple of treats, Maggie devoured a turkey and Swiss sandwich on the last two pieces of rye bread. As soon as she cleaned up her dishes, she donned her coat, grabbed her purse and notebook, and headed out the front door with purpose in every step.

· · · · · · · · · · · · · · · ·

From behind her steering wheel, Maggie soaked in the local scenery as she passed the Oceanview Hotel, Ina's house, and the bed-and-breakfast before pulling up in front of a quaint yellow-and-white Victorian home. If the house hinted of the woman inside, Cynthia Moorman would be stately yet warm and inviting.

Maggie brushed her hair from her face, draped her purse strap over her shoulder, and opened the car door with anticipation. She crossed the sidewalk and pushed on the gate. Perhaps the answers to her questions were waiting at the end of the narrow walkway.

The wind still blew Maggie's hair every which way, but the sun poked hopefully through the clouds. As she climbed the three steps onto the porch, the sun's rays brought life to a stained glass Tree of Knowledge depicted in deep greens and browns set against a sunny blue sky. Maggie, mesmerized by the glass artwork, startled when the door opened.

"May I help you?" The woman who stood in the doorway was regal with an open smile, warm brown eyes, and silver hair pulled back with a navy blue ribbon that matched her sweater.

"Are you Cynthia Moorman?"

The woman nodded. "I am."

"I'm Maggie Watson. I own Carriage House Antiques. My friend Ruth Harper suggested I see you."

"Ah, you're Evelyn Bradbury's niece. I'm happy to meet you. Ruth mentioned you might stop by."

"I'm not sure if she told you, but I purchased some antiques from the Twisdem Mansion auction, and I always enjoy having background about the pieces I sell. Ruth thought you could help."

Cynthia opened the door wider. "Please come in, though I don't know how much help I can be." She led Maggie a few paces through the hallway and into a formal but cozy living room where a fire blazed in the fireplace below a portrait of a stunning woman who looked much like Cynthia but was dressed in conservative, early-twentieth-century clothing.

"She's beautiful," Maggie said, gazing at the portrait. "You resemble her."

"My grandmother. My mother always said I took after her in both appearance and temperament." The older woman chuckled and motioned for Maggie to sit on the floral Victorian love seat.

After Maggie was seated, Cynthia sat in a coordinating wingback chair adjacent to it and crossed her ankles. "Now, what would you like to know about the Twisdem family?"

Maggie chose her words carefully. "They have kept a low profile in town since the accident, so not too many people around town remember much about Scott. I understand you dated him in high school."

Cynthia's eyes softened. "He was my first love. We dated our junior and much of our senior years. Everyone thought we'd get married. I thought he was my soul mate. That's teenage romance for you."

The fire crackled under the carved wood mantel. Maggie waited for Cynthia to continue.

"I broke up with him and returned his class ring." Cynthia's words were quiet, yet they filled the air. "I always regretted it. I hurt him, and then . . ." Her words dissipated into the air like sparks in the fireplace.

"The accident happened," Maggie finished for her. "Why did you break up?"

Cynthia stared into the flames. "When we started dating, Scott wanted to go to art school. His father insisted he go to an Ivy League college and take over the Twisdem business empire. His parents didn't want us to marry so young." She inhaled deeply and slowly let the breath go. "During our senior year, the Vietnam War was a hot issue. His friend Will Rackelman pulled him into the protests. Scott began spending more time protesting with Will than he did with me. My dad served bravely in World War II and Korea. I couldn't condone the protests."

"Sometimes friends can have a bad influence," Maggie said, trying to sound understanding.

"Scott and Will had been friends since childhood. When we were dating, Scott did his best to balance the two relationships. As we spent more time together, Will started hanging out with Philip Johns. Philip played with a local garage band and taught Will how to play the guitar. Will idolized him." Cynthia cleared her throat. "Philip enlisted as soon as he graduated. Three months later, he was killed in Vietnam. I don't think Will ever got over it. He became obsessed with protesting the war and badgered Scott to go with him to rallies."

"Where is Will now?"

Cynthia shrugged. "I don't know. He disappeared around the same time as the car crash. Nobody's heard from him since. His family ran a notice in the paper offering a reward for information leading to his return home, but I don't think anything came of it."

The sorrow in Cynthia's voice sent a wave of guilt through Maggie. "I'm sorry for dredging up a sad part of your life."

"I have happy memories of Scott too. I like remembering them, but you must take the good with the bad." Cynthia smiled. "I've had a wonderful life. God chose Carleton for my husband and we've had a loving marriage. Alzheimer's disease is taking its toll on him, though. I fear soon I'll have no choice but to move him into Fair Winds Nursing Home." She gestured to a table filled with framed photos. "These are our kids and grandkids."

"You have a beautiful family."

"Thank you."

Maggie stood. "I've imposed on you long enough. You've been very gracious."

"It was my pleasure." Cynthia rose from her seat and led Maggie to the front door.

"Thank you for your time," Maggie said.

"And thank you for the visit." Cynthia placed a hand on Maggie's arm. "I hope I've helped you."

"You have." Maggie pulled a business card from the side pocket of her purse and handed it to Cynthia. "Here's my card. Please call me if you'd like to chat again."

Maggie crossed the porch and considered Cynthia's story as she followed the walkway to the Jetta. So many lives had been changed on that January night in 1970. As soon as she unlocked the door and slid behind the wheel, her cell phone alerted her that she had received a text. She started the engine and read the message as the car heated.

Her heart swelled when she saw that the text was from James. He wrote: *I've got a surprise for your research. Busy Bean at 9 a.m. tomorrow? Have lunch meeting in Portland but can meet beforehand.*

Typing as fast as her fingers could go, Maggie responded: *Can't wait, see you then!*

When her phone chimed again, she quickly looked at the display, doing a double take when she saw that it was June, not James, who sent the message this time. *Fedora Man wanted to buy Twisdem items! Told him they weren't priced and I could call him when they are ready. He left in a huff without leaving name or card.*

"Wow, people are obsessed with this family," Maggie whispered, texting her reply to June: *Very odd. Do you need me to come back? I can get roses some other time.*

June's response was almost instantaneous. *I'm fine. Take your time.*

As she pulled away from the curb, Maggie caught a glimpse of movement between the three evergreen trees in Cynthia's side yard. She blinked and looked again. It was gone. She shivered and pulled away from the curb. *What next?*

5

Preoccupied with thoughts of the Twisdems, Maggie nearly collided with James on her way into The Busy Bean the next morning.

"Earth to Maggie. Come in, Maggie." James waved his left hand slowly back and forth in front of Maggie's distant gaze as they both approached the café door at the same time. He held a hardcover book under his other arm.

"Oh!" Maggie's cheeks burned. "I didn't see you."

"You looked like you were on another planet," he said, gently moving her away from the door as he opened it. "Are you all right?"

Maggie stepped into the café with James right behind her. "I was lost in my thoughts, I guess."

"Care to share them?" He led them to his favorite table and pulled out a chair for Maggie.

"Sure, after we have our coffee in hand." She stifled a yawn as she sat down, and James took the seat across from her.

Before he could respond, Daisy bustled up to the table with a coffeepot in one hand and two yellow-and-black striped mugs in the other. "Looks like I arrived just in time. How about a bit of Jamaican blend? It'll wake you up."

Maggie watched the coffeepot spout as Daisy filled one cup and then the other without breaking the stream of liquid or spilling a drop. "Sounds heavenly."

"I aim to please." Daisy set the pot on the table and wiped her brow. "You came at a good time. It was wild in here during breakfast. The buzz was all about the Twisdem Mansion and wondering when you'll have the pieces you bought at the auction up for sale."

"Soon," Maggie said.

"Fantastic. You'll have a crowd when word gets out." Daisy surveyed the room. "Looks like I'm needed in the kitchen. Want anything else? A cinnamon scone, perhaps?"

"Not for me," Maggie said. "I ate breakfast with Snickers this morning."

James shook his head. "Just the coffee for me too. I have an early lunch appointment, so I'll be good."

Daisy winked. "Y'all just holler if you want a refill."

James nodded to Daisy but waited until she was out of earshot to speak. "So, what has you walking around in a daze? It's not like you."

"I didn't sleep well. I guess the Twisdem story has me all twisted up like everyone else. And a few weird things have happened at the manor and shop since the auction."

James's eyebrows lifted and his blue-gray eyes filled with concern. "What kind of things?"

Maggie described the mysterious arrival of the box filled with records and other items she suspected came from the Twisdem Mansion. "Sometimes people leave stuff outside if the shop is closed or they are emotional about letting them go, but usually they will leave a note or business card," Maggie explained. "Rarely are items left without any sort of identification."

James took a drink of coffee and set his mug on the table. "Is that all?"

"When I returned from the historical society meeting that night, I couldn't get the records out of my mind. I guess they reminded me of my dad as much as the Twisdem mystery. I set up the record player in the library." Reluctant to say more, Maggie hesitated.

"And?" James prompted.

She told him about the music and how it brought back

memories of dancing with her father, her feet on top of his, in the living room when she was a little girl. "I listened to song after song. The music was really good."

"Doesn't sound creepy to me," James said.

Maggie dabbed her napkin on her lips to stall. "I was flipping the Simon and Garfunkel album, and I heard a noise at the window. When I turned, I saw eyes looking in at me."

"Man or woman?"

"Not sure. When I stepped to the window, the person, if that's what it was, disappeared into the shadows."

"I don't suppose you called the police."

Maggie squirmed under James's gaze. "No, because . . ."

"You didn't want to bother them because you weren't hurt and nothing was stolen."

It sounded silly when James said it, but he was right. "Something like that."

He took a deep breath and shook his head. "What am I going to do with you?"

Time to change the subject. "Well, for starters, you could show me the book you brought with you."

James laughed and reached for the hardcover tome. "Very smooth. But for my peace of mind, will you please report the incident to the police so they have a record of it?"

"Maybe."

"You're incorrigible, you know that?" He pushed the book across the turquoise tabletop. "I have a present for you. I found it years ago in a used bookstore."

"*Somerset Harbor Mansions and Their Families.*" Maggie read the title aloud and turned to the copyright page. "Published in 1968. When Scott Twisdem was in high school."

"The Twisdem Mansion is on page fifty-two. I think you'll find it interesting." James peered at his watch. "But right now

I need to get on the road to Portland for my meeting. Huge restoration project."

Maggie stood up, clutching the volume. "This will be a big help." She pushed her chair under the table with her hip.

James cupped his hand around Maggie's elbow and led her to the cash register. "You know, you should give Pop Welborn a call if you're interested in anything that happened at the high school in the last sixty years."

Maggie had forgotten about Pop. "I met him soon after I moved to Somerset Harbor. You're right. His memory is astounding. And he's quite a character. I'll call him this afternoon."

James pulled out his wallet as Daisy appeared behind the register. "This morning is on me."

Daisy handed James his change, then turned to Maggie. "I'm sorry I got busy in the kitchen and didn't get back to you. But I want an update on the Twisdem estate as soon as you learn anything."

James chuckled. "I think the entire town wants an update."

"You got it." Daisy winked. "Come back soon with some info."

"I will," Maggie said as James opened the door.

When they were out on the sidewalk, James stared at Maggie with an intensity that made her wonder if she had a smudge on her face. "Please tell the police about the Peeping Tom, Maggie. You mean a lot to a lot of people around here, and I'm one of them."

. . . .

The phone rang twice. "Pop Welborn here." His tone was a mixture of military precision and cheer.

"Mr. Wel—"

"We agreed you'd call me Pop, remember?" Maggie imagined his eyes were twinkling. "Or I'll be forced to call you Mrs. Watson, and I think we're beyond formality, don't you?"

"Yes, Pop, I agree."

"What can I do for you, young lady?"

Maggie laughed. "I don't get called 'young lady' very often."

"Well, when you get to be my age, you earn the right to call most people young." In his midnineties, Pop was a rather spry veteran of World War II. He had a point.

"I'm researching the Twisdem family, and a little birdie reminded me that you are an expert when it comes to Somerset Harbor history. Do you have time for a visit tomorrow?"

"I can always fit you into my schedule, Maggie."

"What time works best for you?"

"Well, let's see." Maggie could picture him lifting his military veteran's cap from his head and rubbing his gnarly hand over the few thin hairs left on his scalp. "I'll be at the VFW Post in the morning. We're planning a fund-raiser for a local military family. The father was wounded in Afghanistan and they're having a tough time." He cleared his throat. "I'll be home by noon. How about two o'clock? That will give me time for a sandwich and a nap."

"Sounds perfect. I'll see you then."

Pop reminded Maggie of his address and she wrote it on the pad of paper she kept on a small desk in the kitchen. After she hung up the phone, Maggie checked the to-do list anchored by a rock with *I Love You* and three lopsided hearts painted on it, a Mother's Day gift made by Emily in elementary school. She perused the list and sighed. Reading about the Twisdem Mansion in the book from James would have to wait. Bill paying and record keeping had to come first.

The sun was setting by the time Maggie checked the items off her to-do list with a sense of satisfaction. After a quick dinner of leftover beef stew, she lit a fire in the library, curled up in her chair, and opened *Somerset Harbor Mansions and*

Their Families. She resisted the urge to read the chapter about Sedgwick Manor and instead flipped the pages until she found the section about Twisdem Mansion. Much of the family history repeated what she had heard, but Maggie was fascinated by paintings done and photographs taken of the mansion during different time periods. The size of the house had doubled over the two centuries since it was built by Scott Twisdem's ancestors. Two wings had been added, one on each side of the house, plus two porches, one along the back of the main house and another along the east side. Maggie was pleased to see some of the furniture pieces she had purchased at the auction shown in the photos.

She was reading about the servants' quarters when her cell phone rang from its perch on the tobacco stand. "Hello?"

"Is this Maggie Watson?" The voice sounded familiar.

"Yes."

"Maggie, this is Cynthia Moorman. I'm sorry to bother you. I didn't know who else to call."

Fear flashed through Maggie. "Cynthia, are you all right?"

"I think so. But ever since you left, I've had the feeling I'm being watched." Cynthia, so calm and friendly during their visit, sounded shaken. "I keep thinking someone is on the porch or out in the yard. It's so unlike me to worry like this."

"Have you called the police?"

"No. What would I tell them? I haven't really seen anyone. I'll sound like a crazy old woman."

She doesn't sound crazy. Maggie paced around the library and bent down to pet Snickers as he walked through the door. "I understand completely."

Maggie stood straight again as Snickers strolled to the rug in front of the fireplace. She hesitated a few moments before telling Cynthia about the face at her library window. "I think you should call the police," she said after recounting her story. "Do you have anyone who can stay with you tonight?"

"I'll call my son and daughter-in-law."

"If you can't reach them, please let me know. We'll figure something out."

"Thank you." Cynthia's voice was calmer now. "Good night."

"Call if I can help. Take care." Maggie sank into her chair and stared into the fire.

What in the world is going on in Somerset Harbor?

6

Maggie stood at the breakfast room window, sipping a cup of coffee and gazing at the sunbeams shining through the trees along the path to the shop. The day was off to a beautiful start, but Maggie had been up since dawn fretting about Cynthia and wondering if her son had been able to stay with her overnight.

It was nearly eight o'clock. Surely Cynthia would be awake by now.

"Please be all right," she whispered as she picked up her cell phone and dialed Cynthia's number.

"Hello?"

Relief surged through Maggie at the sound of Cynthia's voice. "Cynthia, this is Maggie Watson. I woke up thinking about your strange experience and wanted to check on you. I hope this isn't too early to call."

"Oh, goodness no. I'm always up with the chickens," Cynthia said. "Everything is fine."

Maggie took a deep breath and exhaled slowly. "So last night was uneventful?"

"Once I calmed down, yes. Isn't it amazing how your mind can blow things out of proportion? I called the police and my son, Travis. I was glad to have him here while Officer Linton took my report. Robert is such a fine young man."

Maggie smiled at the word "young." She and Robert Linton were about the same age. "He's a nice guy."

"Excuse me a moment." Cynthia's voice was muffled for several seconds. "I'm sorry. My son spent the night and he was asking me if I wanted more coffee."

"I won't keep you. I'm just happy to know you're all right."

"You were kind to check on me. Thank you. I'll let you know if anything else happens."

"Please do. Bye now." Maggie hung up the phone and strolled to the master suite closet, where she picked out jeans and a teal pullover. Knowing Cynthia was safe would allow her to concentrate on her day's other appointments. When she was dressed, she headed to the shop to help June prepare space for the furniture purchased at the Twisdem Mansion before her appointment with Pop.

. . . .

Pop's home with his granddaughter, Dani Freemont, was a tidy clapboard cottage perched on the outskirts of town. The door opened as Maggie lifted her hand to rap on it.

"You're right on time, Maggie. I like that." Pop opened the door wider and motioned her inside.

He was a wonder. Although his tall, thin frame was stoop-shouldered, his voice was strong and his mind quick and accurate. His memory amazed Maggie. The old man recalled facts, figures, and faces better than she did.

"I heard you were a stickler for punctuality."

"Ah, you must have been talking to my former pupils." Pop's gray eyes twinkled. "I was notorious for sending students to the office when they were tardy."

Maggie pretended to turn a lock on her lips as she had when Emily had shared a secret as a child. "I'll never tell."

"You're punctual and principled." Pop led her into a small living room with a plaid sofa facing a large picture window. "Please take a seat on the sofa. My creaky old bones require the recliner."

Maggie complied and found herself sitting in front of a tray that held a plate of heart-shaped sugar cookies, two mugs, several Valentine's Day napkins, and an insulated carafe.

"My granddaughter, Dani, fixed us a snack. She's sequestered herself in the den to get some work done. She's a medical transcriptionist." He nodded at the tray. "She bakes special cookies for every holiday. There's hot cocoa in the carafe."

"The cookies look delicious." Maggie reached for a cup. "May I do the honors?"

"Please do. Then we'll get down to business."

Maggie poured a cup of thick hot chocolate and placed one cup on the accent table next to Pop along with two cookies on a napkin. Then she served herself.

"Mmmm, this is homemade, isn't it?" Maggie inhaled the aroma before sipping the cocoa. "It's heavenly."

"Indeed it is. Dani doesn't believe in mixes," Pop said with pride in his voice. "So, how may I help you?"

Maggie told him about the auction at the Twisdem Mansion and her curiosity about the family.

"I like to have information to give our customers when they purchase antiques. People are particularly interested in items from the mansion," she said, reaching for another cookie. "I talked to Cynthia Moorman. She told me about Scott Twisdem and his friendship with Will Rackelman and Philip Johns. I'd like to know more about them."

Pop picked up a cookie and pointed it toward the large bookcase that nearly covered the far end of the room. "Look on those shelves for the 1968 Somerset Harbor yearbook and bring it to me, please. I'll put faces to the names for you. All three boys should be in that one."

Maggie walked to the massive bookcase and searched thirty-five years' worth of yearbooks dating to 1951. She found 1968 on the end of the second shelf. "Here it is," she said, removing the volume.

She placed the book on Pop's lap, afraid its weight would be too much for his fragile arms. Maggie stood beside his chair as he opened the yearbook and flipped through. He stopped in the middle of the book and pointed to a grinning kid with unruly blond hair. "Here's your Mr. Rackelman. He was a good kid. Average student. Outgoing. He turned out to be a pretty good musician. Family was well-off but not in the same league as the Twisdems."

"And Scott Twisdem?"

The teacher's finger moved down a row and over one. "This is Scott. He was a handsome young man, smart, artistic. Girls called him 'dreamy' and drooled over his brown hair and eyes. He was more introspective than Will but sociable. They were thick as thieves until Scott fell in puppy love."

"What happened?"

"You know teenagers. They fall fast and hard. Scott spent more of his free time with his girl, and Will found a new friend and guitar teacher in Philip Johns." He flipped to the senior class page and pointed to a boy whose hair was probably long enough to have flaunted the school rules. "Philip was smart but his grades didn't reflect it. He was more interested in practicing with his garage band than doing homework. But kids thought he was cool, including Scott and Will."

"Philip graduated and enlisted, right?"

Pop nodded. "He didn't have much of a choice. His parents didn't have the means to send him to college. Jobs were scarce around here, so he signed on with the Army. I think his parents encouraged it. His father had served in World War II."

"How did Will and Scott react when Philip was killed in Vietnam?"

The old man seemed lost in thought for a minute, then shook himself out of it. "It was a turbulent time. There was constant talk of the draft lottery, and antiwar protests were common. Philip's death pushed Will into activism. In class, if called on to answer a question, he'd find a way to turn his reply into an antiwar statement. He began cutting school to hitchhike to New York City and Boston to protest."

"Did Scott skip school to go with him?"

Pop squeezed his eyes shut in concentration. "I think so. Sometimes, maybe. It was a long time ago. Keep in mind, too, that the Twisdems were all about appearance. They wouldn't let Scott do anything that would ruin their plans for him—Harvard and the family business."

Maggie looked out the window. Shadows lengthened across the tiny front lawn. "You've been generous with your time. Thank you." She stood. "My father is flying in for a visit tomorrow night, and I need to get a few things ready for him."

The old man rose to his feet. "My pleasure. Come back anytime."

"Be careful, I might take you up on that," Maggie said.

"I certainly hope so." Pop opened the front door. "Maybe next time Dani will be able to join us."

Maggie was halfway to the car when a text arrived from June: *Twisdem items arrived safe & sound. Gorgeous!*

. . . .

Maggie's mind whirled with thoughts of Pop Welborn's stories as she pulled clean sheets, pillowcases, and towels from the closet in the guest suite the following evening. She hung a fresh set of towels in the guest bathroom, then carried the sheets and pillowcases into the bedroom.

She hummed "Amazing Grace" as she smoothed down the corners of the paisley fitted sheet and spread the matching flat sheet on top of it. As soon as she arranged the burgundy bedspread across the bed, Snickers jumped in the middle of it.

"Making sure it's comfortable, are you?" she asked the cat, who'd begun to groom himself. He ignored her and continued to lick his paw.

Maggie slid a fresh case onto the pillow and fluffed it. Satisfied with the room, she trotted down the stairs, then stepped outside on a whim. As she did, she heard a banging sound and then breaking glass coming from the direction of the shop. She stopped short, her arm hair standing on end.

Maggie dashed back inside, grabbed her pepper spray from the kitchen desk, and ran out the side door toward the shop. As soon as she cleared the trees, she saw a man run to a vehicle and peel out of the parking lot. Maggie pursued him to the end of the driveway, but she couldn't see the make of the car or get a license plate number.

Maggie approached the shop and walked around the exterior. She found the broken window in back. Looking down, she also discovered a dark scarf on the ground. Her stunned mind repeated a single thought over and over.

Someone just tried to break into my shop.

. . . .

Standing in the foyer, Officer Janeen Crosby raised her eyebrows. "Let me get this straight. You chased after the man?"

"I did, and I would have soaked him with pepper spray if I'd been fast enough."

Officer Crosby shook her head, and the bangs of her short hairstyle slid down her forehead. "As many times as we've been to this house, you still try to take matters into your own hands."

Maggie blushed. Officer Crosby was right. The Somerset Harbor Police Department had been called to Sedgwick Manor an embarrassing number of times since Maggie moved in. Mysteries kept riding in on antiques. "Just call me the problem child."

Robert Linton, who'd been searching the property while Officer Crosby finished taking the report, walked in the front door just in time to hear her.

"I wouldn't go that far." Officer Linton appeared to be restraining a chuckle, which made his boyish freckled face look much younger than his forty-odd years. "But it's hard to keep you safe if you insist on chasing after burglars."

"I couldn't just sit here and do nothing."

"Know what you *could* do?" Officer Crosby pushed the slender notepad into her back pocket and then crossed her arms over her chest. "Stay in your house and call 911 instead."

"She's right." Robert gave Maggie a hard look. "You really should be more cautious. I've checked the entire property and bagged the scarf in case this guy returns. The window will need to be replaced, but I didn't see any other damage."

Officer Crosby chimed in. "We'll send a patrol to drive by every hour or so—"

The doorbell rang and the two officers exchanged looks. "Expecting someone so late?" Robert asked. "It's after ten o'clock."

Maggie's hand went to her cheek. "Oh, yes I am. In all the excitement, I totally forgot." Feeling guilty, she opened the door to find her father bathed in the soft glow of the porch light.

"Dad, I'm so glad you're here." She stepped onto the porch and hugged him around the neck.

"Me too, Mags." Neil broke away from the embrace and held her out at arm's length for a moment, his face beaming. He backed up and drew a tall, broad-shouldered woman from the shadows surrounding the porch. "Maggie," he said, wrapping one arm around the Amazonian stranger, "I'd like you to meet Daphne Bergman. My fiancée."

Maggie stared at the woman and blinked as if she had seen an apparition. "Fiancée?" She looked at her father. "You're getting married?"

The silence was deafening until a nervous cough came from inside the house. "Excuse me, Mrs. Watson?" Officer Crosby appeared in the doorway. "We have everything we need. We'll let you know if we have any updates."

Maggie moved to give the officers room to get by. "Thank you for responding so quickly."

"We aim to serve." Officer Linton followed his partner onto the porch as Maggie's father and his fiancée shuffled aside, their faces wrinkled in confusion. Robert turned to Maggie, his face devoid of his customary smile. "Next time, leave the pursuit to us." He followed his partner down the front steps and past two large rolling suitcases on the edge of the walkway.

Pivoting away from the officers, Maggie motioned her father and his fiancée inside and closed the door.

"So, Maggie, are you going to explain what we walked into here?" Her father was using the same tone he saved for disciplinary lectures when she was a child.

"Of course," she said. *You have some explaining of your own to do.* She needed time to process their engagement news. "Let's get you settled into your rooms first, and then we can swap news." Thank goodness Emily's room was clean. Daphne could stay in there.

"You two go on up and I'll grab the suitcases," Neil said. "It's been a long time since I've been in Sedgwick Manor, but I think I can find the way."

"We'll meet you upstairs." Panic flashed through Maggie as he walked out the front door. What would she say to this woman, her father's surprise fiancée?

"Right this way." Maggie led the way to the grand staircase. "Welcome to Sedgwick Manor, Daphne." When they reached the top, she strode to the first door at the top of the stairs. "This is my daughter, Emily's, bedroom. She's away at college. You'll have your own bathroom and walk-in closet." Maggie pushed the door open, flipped a light switch, and walked to the center of the room. "The bottom two drawers of the bureau are empty, so feel free to use them."

Daphne took several paces into the room and turned around in slow motion. "Oh, what a delightful bedroom. I love the wisteria wallpaper."

Maggie smiled in spite of her reservations. "So does Emily." *Surely that's a good sign.*

Shuffling noises filtered down the hallway. A moment later, Maggie's father deposited a navy blue suitcase outside the doorway and pulled a deep purple rolling bag into the room. "The house looks fantastic, Maggie. It must be a lot for one person to handle."

"It keeps me busy, but Aunt Evelyn arranged for the house and grounds upkeep to continue after she was gone." She cleared her throat. "I have you set up in the guest suite, Dad."

"The room with the balcony? I remember it well." He backed out of the room, suitcase in hand, and walked down the hallway.

"Daphne, the bathroom is through there," said Maggie, nodding to a door across the room. "You and Dad can freshen up if you want. I'll meet you downstairs in the breakfast room. I'm sure he remembers where it is."

. . . .

Thoughts bounced around Maggie's mind as she sliced an apple and what remained of a small brick of cheese to add to the light snack tray she'd prepared for her father's arrival. It was nearing eleven o'clock, but she knew that traveling always made her father hungry, no matter what time it was. Serving food would also give her a chance to find out more about this woman who was apparently to become her stepmother. *Why hasn't Dad told me about this relationship until now?*

She put the teakettle on the stove, arranged a variety of herbal tea bags in a small bowl, and lined up three mugs and spoons on the counter. While the water heated, Maggie took several napkins and the cheese-and-fruit tray to the breakfast room table. The kettle whistled as Neil and Daphne walked hand in hand into the breakfast room.

They were an interesting couple. At nearly six feet, Maggie's father wasn't short, but Daphne had a good three inches on him. The height difference didn't seem to bother either one of them, though. Her father radiated the same calming presence she remembered, while Daphne was the picture of energy, with sparkling eyes and a bright smile.

"Maggie, you're sweet to fix us a midnight snack." Daphne looked around the kitchen. "My stomach started growling as soon as we walked off the plane, but we didn't want to waste any time getting here."

"You're welcome." Maggie ushered them to the counter where she'd left the mugs. She turned off the stove and moved the kettle to another burner. "I have a selection of teas, or I can brew some decaf coffee. Do you need cream or sugar?"

Her father put an arm around her shoulder and squeezed gently. "This is fine."

They each fixed a cup of tea and carried it to the table. Anticipation overwhelmed Maggie, who couldn't wait much longer to learn more about this woman in her father's life.

Neil blew on his tea, causing the steam to swirl away from him. "I'm ready to hear why we arrived to find police at your door."

Maggie sighed. Her questions would have to wait, it would seem.

"Not much to tell. It happened so fast." She recounted an abridged version of what she'd told the police. "Par for the course when you own a business. Everything will be fine. Now it's your turn. How and when did you two meet?"

"Well, we, um . . ." Maggie's father stammered, a hint of red tinting his cheeks.

"Dad, I don't think I've ever seen you blush." Maggie smiled.

"Oh, there's nothing to be embarrassed about, Neil, honey." Daphne patted his leg and left her hand resting on his knee. "Plenty of people go line dancing."

"You met where?" Maggie looked from her father's face to Daphne's. "Did you say line dancing?"

"I did. My feet had bruises to prove it." Daphne tapped her feet on the tile to make her point.

Neil covered Daphne's hand with his. "Both of us had our fair share of bruised toes. We were equally bad, weren't we?"

Daphne laughed. "We couldn't keep in step."

"But it gave us a good excuse to go outside to sit in the quiet and talk," he said. "The hoedown was a fund-raiser for Hearts and Horses, a nonprofit offering art experiences and horseback riding for children and adults with special needs. We're both volunteers. I'm their financial adviser and Daphne is an instructor."

Maggie's heart sank. She knew so little of her father's life in Michigan. Dancing. Volunteering. What else was she missing? "I didn't know you were volunteering."

"We gave up the dancing while we still have four left feet between us," Daphne said, grinning. "But we've found plenty else to do. I taught him to paint. He introduced me to fly-fishing."

"I see we have a lot to talk about while you're here." Maggie stifled a yawn. "I'm sorry. I'm not bored by any means. It's just been a long day, not to mention a strange night."

"We should let you get some sleep," her father said. He squeezed Daphne's hand. "Maggie's always been an 'early to bed and early to rise' person."

They all stood and Maggie hugged her father. "I'm glad you're here." When he released her, Maggie turned to Daphne and searched for the right words. "I'm looking forward to getting to know you."

Her father's fiancée beamed at her. "You and me both, Maggie."

. . . .

Maggie ran the sponge back and forth over the surface of the frying pan, rinsed it under the faucet, and handed it to her father. "You're getting domesticated in your old age," she said lightly as he dried the pan and set it in the dish drainer. "Look at you doing dishes after you helped make breakfast."

"I didn't have much choice after your mother died. She took good care of me, so I had to learn a lot of new things when she was gone. I do laundry now too."

But did you have to learn them in Michigan? Silence hung between them. Daphne had gone upstairs to get dressed while they cleaned the breakfast dishes, and this was Maggie's chance to ask the question that had nagged her since her mother's death. "Dad, why did you move to Michigan so soon after Mom died?"

Neil's eyes filled with tears, but they didn't fall. "I was devastated when I lost your mother. Each morning, I had a harder time getting out of bed and facing the day. Food wasn't appetizing. I couldn't enjoy reading or fishing." He looked away, grabbed the sponge, and wiped water droplets from the faucet. "You had enough on your plate with your own grief while taking care of Richard and Emily. You didn't need to worry about me too."

Maggie emptied out the dishwater and watched the bubbles swirl down the drain. "But you were so far away. It felt like I lost my mother and father at the same time."

Neil wrapped his arms around Maggie and pulled her close. "I'm so sorry, Mags. I never meant it to feel like that. I was in such a bad way, and I didn't want to be a burden to you."

"You wouldn't have been a burden, Dad."

Daphne's bootheels sounded against the kitchen floor. "After that delicious woodchopper's breakfast and a hot shower, I'm ready to get the grand tour of this charming town of yours." She stopped short. "Am I interrupting something?"

"No, you're fine." Maggie stepped away from her father and wiped her eyes as she turned to switch off the coffeepot. "I'm ready when you are," she said.

. . . .

"Oh, Maggie, Somerset Harbor is a beautiful town." Daphne appeared to be completely charmed by Old Faith Chapel, the iconic lighthouse, and the mansions sprawling along Shoreline Drive. "It has the same feel as Lapeer, Michigan—stately and homey at the same time."

Much to Maggie's initial disappointment, her father had insisted Daphne sit up front so she could see the sights as they toured Somerset Harbor. She'd hoped her father would be her copilot, but Maggie found herself enjoying Daphne's enthusiasm.

"Did you grow up in Lapeer?" Maggie was curious about this woman who'd put life back into her father's eyes. Daphne was turning out to be an exuberant conversationalist and an open book.

"I've lived there my whole life, except for two years at art school in Chicago." Daphne's head turned from side to side as they drove down Wharf Road. "When I came home for the summer after my sophomore year, I met Gus at the Asparagus Festival and decided not to return to Chicago. Six months later, we married and moved to his family's farm outside of town."

Maggie stole a glance at her father's fiancée. Daphne's cropped salt-and-pepper hair framed her face, but the most noticeable feature was the wide smile above the angular chin. She exuded joy.

"Where do you live now?"

"Oh, I'm still on the farm. My son and daughter each have homes on the property, and between them, I have four grand-children running around."

"You must love having them so close." Maggie looked in the rearview mirror, but she couldn't see her father's face. Did he ever wish he lived closer to his daughter and granddaughter? After their conversation that morning, she was sure he did.

"I love seeing my grandkids every day." Daphne chuckled. "I traded my cow herding and tractor riding for babysitting and giving art lessons. My family has kept me busy since Gus died, God rest his soul."

Maggie heard her father whisper something to his fiancée from the back seat. Daphne cleared her throat, then said, "Your dad is selling his place in town and moving to the farm after we're married."

Maggie tried to picture her father on a farm. "That'll be . . . an interesting change."

The sun was shining, and the temperature was an unseasonably warm forty-eight degrees. The snow from the previous week was long gone and more folks than usual strolled the sidewalks. Maggie pulled her car into a parking lot a couple of blocks down from The Busy Bean. "It's beautiful outside, so I thought we could walk a couple of blocks and look at the shops on our way to The Busy Bean."

The trio meandered down the streets, stopping when Daphne declared, "I just gotta see this place," which happened outside the art gallery, the Nautical Scribe bookstore, the craft co-op, and The Quilt Cupboard. During their walk, Maggie made a discovery about Daphne: While not as refined and formally educated as Maggie's mother had been, Daphne was well-read and intelligent, and she knew a lot about art.

But Maggie still felt a stab of pain in her heart as she watched Neil and Daphne stroll hand in hand down the sidewalk. *How could Dad replace Mom, especially with a woman so different?*

After exiting The Quilt Cupboard, Maggie realized her stomach was growling. "Why don't we stop for lunch? The Busy Bean is just across the street."

"That sounds great. My stomach has rumbled for two blocks," Neil said.

Daphne gazed toward the café and smiled. "It's adorable. Look at the logo. The bee is dive-bombing the coffee."

They hurried across the street and found The Busy Bean buzzing with activity. Standing away from the register area, they waited as Jenny, a server, cleared the dirty dishes from a recently vacated table. Daphne surveyed the room, her eyes widening when she saw Daisy's Miss Savannah sash and crown displayed on the wall. "Is this place run by a beauty queen?"

As if on cue, Daisy approached them on her way to the register. "Hi, Maggie. Jenny is about to finish up, so hang tight." She smiled at Maggie's father and Daphne. "You must be Maggie's dad. I see the resemblance."

Maggie's father smiled. "I am, and this is my fiancée, Daphne Bergman."

Daisy cut her eyes to Maggie for a second before extending her hand first to Daphne and then to Neil. "Happy to meet you. I need to man the register, but I'll try to get by your table to visit with you."

After Daisy moved to the register, Maggie explained how Daisy won the coffee shop years ago in an essay competition held by the former owners.

"She certainly has style." Daphne eyed the crown wistfully. "The most I ever won was the Asparagus Queen title when I was seventeen."

Maggie heard her name called and looked toward the register, where Daisy was pointing at the front window. "Your table is ready, folks."

Maggie led her father and Daphne through the crowded room. Two tables from the window, she spied a familiar face: Still wearing his fedora, the mysterious bidder from the Twisdem Mansion was in a heated argument with a stocky bald man. Maggie stood still, her eyes fixed on the quarreling men. Fedora Man, a gray ponytail hanging below the brim of his hat, slammed his fist on the table, then jumped up and knocked over his chair. With a table beside her and Daphne behind her, Maggie couldn't move out of the way as he approached. Head down and fists clenched, the angry man bumped into her without seeming to see her as he stormed out of the coffee shop.

Maggie and several of the other patrons gaped after him. *What was that all about?*

Neil flipped through the records on top of the library desk and let out a long whistle. "This is quite a collection you have here."

Happiness coursed through Maggie as she watched him from her favorite chair. "I knew you'd like them." She waited for him to get to the very last album before saying any more.

"I can't believe it!" He pulled the remaining album from the box and gazed at it. He flipped it over and studied the back, amazement and delight on his face. "Cole Loveren. An original of his first album, *Apparition*." Neil looked from Maggie to Daphne, then lifted the record in reverence. "Let's listen to this one."

"The record player is behind you on the table under the window," Maggie said, absently stroking the top of Snickers's head.

Maggie watched her father ease the old vinyl record onto the turntable and set the needle in place. Years fell from his face when the music filled the library. Neil sat next to Daphne and sang along, tentatively at first, then growing stronger with each verse. When the first song ended, he asked, "Where in the world did you find this?"

"It came to us, actually." Maggie carried Snickers across the room and stood by her father. She hesitated, unsure of how much to tell him. "The records were in a box with a bunch of other items left outside the shop last week. My shop manager, June, found them."

"Someone discarded a whole box of music history?" His eyes widened. "Incredible."

"June wanted to take them to a thrift store, but I knew you would like them. I had planned to send them for your birthday, but giving them to you in person is even better." Maggie looked out the window at the afternoon sun, shivering as she recalled the eyes she thought she had seen there when she played the records.

"Mags?" Her father waved his hand in front of Maggie's face. "What's wrong?"

Maggie blinked. "What? Oh, nothing. I was thinking of what happened while I was listening to Simon and Garfunkel the other night."

"You look positively spooked." Daphne walked to the window and gazed outside a moment before turning to face Maggie. "What aren't you telling us?"

"It's nothing. Really." Maggie squirmed. *What if I imagined the face at the window?*

Daphne put her arm around Maggie's shoulder and led her to one of the fireside chairs. "Your father's concerned. Quite frankly, so am I. We arrive to find the police at your door, then you're practically assaulted at the coffee shop, and now you look like you've seen a ghost."

"No ghost. I saw a perfectly corporeal pair of eyes at the window. Someone watched me play the records, but he didn't try to get in the house. If it was a he, and not just an animal." Maggie felt ridiculous. "And the man at the coffee shop has almost nothing to do with me. I'm fine."

Her father paced back and forth in front of the fireplace. "You need to install an alarm system in the house and the shop. It's not safe for you to be in this big house all alone."

"Neil, dear, she doesn't need an alarm," Daphne said. "She needs a husband."

Mortified, Maggie took a few deep breaths and then changed the subject. "Why don't I fix some tea?" She stood and slipped around her father's fiancée. "I'll be right back."

"I'll come with you." Daphne followed her to the library door. "You can't carry three cups of steaming-hot tea."

As they entered the foyer, Daphne emitted a squeal of delight so intense that Maggie stopped in her tracks.

"Just look at how that chandelier sparkles in the sun!" Her head thrown back, Daphne gazed at the light with adoring eyes.

"It really is something, isn't it?" Maggie took a moment to admire it herself.

"I mean, I noticed it last night, certainly. But today, in the sunlight, it's positively radiant," Daphne said as Neil stepped into the foyer. "None of the venues we've looked at for the wedding are half as beautiful as Sedgwick Manor, are they, honey?"

"That's true." Neil smirked, then said lightly, "Maybe we should just get married here."

Daphne squealed again and clutched his arm. "I know you're joking, but . . . maybe we should?" She turned to Maggie. "This is just about as presumptuous as you can get, but what would you think about having the wedding here, at Sedgwick Manor?"

Maggie looked at her blankly, barely processing the request, so Daphne continued. "Our families can't agree on a location, and Neil and I have been talking about eloping all along anyway. Why not do it here in this beautiful manor?"

"Well, nothing would make me happier than to get married in my daughter's home." Neil swept Daphne into a hug and kissed her cheek, then turned to Maggie. "But I certainly wouldn't want to impose."

Maggie struggled to collect her thoughts and control her breathing. *How did this happen?* One second she was on her way to the kitchen to fix tea, and the next she was being asked to host her father's wedding to a woman she'd met less than twenty-four hours ago. She asked the first thing that came to mind. "When did you want to get married?"

"Let's do it while we're here now. Just skip the guest list entirely and only have us." Daphne wrapped her arms around Neil and looked down at him. "It will be perfect, won't it? We'll have the most incredible Valentine's Day wedding."

"Valentine's Day?" Maggie's voice cracked. Her father was beaming. Daphne was all smiles. But Maggie couldn't think straight. Everything was happening too fast.

Daphne looked like a blushing young bride-to-be instead of a retired farmer in her midsixties. "I just know it could be fabulous."

Maggie walked to the stairway and sat on the third step. "You want to plan a wedding here? In one week?"

"We're not talking about a big to-do, Mags." Her father disentangled himself from his fiancée and sat down next to Maggie. "All we need are you, Emily, and a minister."

"And maybe some other nice touches. And a marriage license. Let's go get that now. I'll grab our coats." Daphne disappeared toward the sunroom.

Maggie's father touched her arm. "Are you okay with this?"

"I want you to be happy, Dad."

"But?"

"It's awfully sudden." She was struck by the tender look on his face. She couldn't disappoint him. "But I do want you to be happy. And if this will make you happy, then I support you."

"And I want you to be happy for me."

"I am, Dad. Truly." Then Maggie grinned. "Is this why your phone calls were so weird?"

Her dad nodded, a sheepish look on his face. "I kept trying to work up the courage to tell you, and then I'd realize I couldn't, so I figured I better do it in person."

The tapping of Daphne's bootheels got louder as she reappeared with two coats in hand. "Let's get that license."

Then they were gone.

. . . .

Maggie was still sitting on the stairs when June called ten minutes later.

"I thought I'd get started sorting and pricing the Twisdem box lots this afternoon," June said. "Do you want to help?"

"I could use the distraction." Maggie stood up and stretched. "I'll be right over."

"Uh-oh. Is your father causing trouble already?"

Maggie groaned. "You have no idea. I'll fill you in when I get there."

"I'm in the back."

After hanging up, Maggie walked through the house and grabbed her coat on her way through the sunroom. The midafternoon sun was beginning its descent to the west as she set off along the path to the shop. She was grateful to have some interesting work to do to keep her occupied while she wrapped her mind around the whole wedding business.

She found June in the back of the shop, surrounded by their spoils from the auction. In addition to several pieces of furniture, there were also two crates full of china and silver they had purchased in box lots.

June stood over the worktable, using a box cutter to carefully slice bubble wrap off of what appeared to be a crystal vase. "What happened with your dad? Everything okay?"

Maggie picked up the packaging material and folded it. "If your definition of 'okay' is Dad arriving with a surprise fiancée in tow at the precise time the police were leaving the manor, I guess everything is all right."

The box cutter clattered to the table. "Fiancée? Police? I don't know which to ask about first."

"You didn't get my message last night?"

June looked sheepish. "I gave my house a good scrubbing

yesterday and fell asleep before nine o'clock. I haven't checked my messages today."

"I'll tell you as we unpack." Maggie reached into the crate and lifted out a wrapped item. She peeled off a layer of bubble wrap to reveal a pair of matching porcelain candlesticks with a floral design.

June took another item from the box. "Start with the police."

"Have you been in the office today?" Maggie set the candlesticks aside and started unwrapping a glass candy dish.

"No. The delivery truck pulled in the same time I did. Between the delivery and customers, I haven't made it to the office."

"You'll find the window covered with plywood, courtesy of my dad." Maggie described hearing the breaking glass, her futile chase of the burglar, and the visit from Officers Linton and Crosby.

"And you're just now telling me?" June stopped and gave her a sharp look. "Maggie, it's three thirty in the afternoon."

Maggie put down the dish she was unwrapping and looked June in the eyes. "I would have kept calling you, but it was late, and then Dad showed up with Daphne, and then today they wanted the full tour of Somerset Harbor. For the grand finale, Daphne asked to have their wedding at Sedgwick Manor. On Valentine's Day. And somehow I agreed."

June put the Dresden figurine she'd just unpacked on the worktable and wrapped her arms around Maggie. "Your life has been crazy for the last twenty-four hours, hasn't it?"

"Daphne was a shock, but having the wedding at the manor in a week is overwhelming. Yesterday I didn't even know the bride existed. Who is this woman Dad wants to marry?" Maggie stepped away from the embrace and lifted her hands in frustration. Her father's news had certainly thrown her off-balance. "On top of everything, I forgot to call Nate Gregory about replacing the broken window."

"I'll take care of it as soon as we finish here. Don't you worry a bit. You have enough on your plate."

"Thank you."

Maggie wandered back to the recently unloaded Twisdem furniture and wished she'd had the funds and space to purchase more. The mansion had been filled with historical treasures.

"Wow, the tiger maple sideboard is even more gorgeous than I remembered." Maggie walked around the piece checking to make sure it wasn't damaged during delivery. She ran the fingers of her left hand down each of the carved pillars flanking the bottom cabinet. "Everything looks good."

"I've never seen one in better condition," June said.

Maggie easily opened the doors and closed them. "This darker inlay border on the top, cabinet, and drawers is handsome. I wonder why they didn't have a matching set. You'd think there'd be a table and chairs, at least. Maybe a china cabinet."

"I think every generation renovates and redecorates old mansions. Even if the sideboard did have companions two hundred years ago, my guess is the rest of the pieces were sacrificed to make way for new furnishings. We'll never know why this one survived." June opened the first of three small drawers lined across the top of the cabinet doors and peered inside.

"What are you looking for?"

"Sometimes the key is hidden in the back of a drawer. Thankfully none of these doors is locked, but it'll add value if we have the key." June pulled on the middle drawer, but it stuck before opening halfway. She bent down to get a closer look and tried to work the drawer open by lifting and pulling it at the same time. The drawer slid out a little more and made a clicking sound. "Aha."

"Did you find the key?" Maggie moved closer to the sideboard and craned her neck to see over June's shoulder.

"Even better. A hidden compartment." June eased the drawer open far enough to see inside the discovery. June pulled out the drawer a bit farther. "Oh good, the key is taped to the side here."

June moved to the side, out of Maggie's way. "Why don't you check the compartment? This piece was your find."

Maggie reached past the outer drawer where the key was taped to the side and patted the interior of the hidden space. Anticipation welled inside her as her fingers felt something. She grasped the items and pulled them from the drawer. In the light, she saw that she held two small pieces of paper, yellowed with age. She examined them, then read aloud, "'Selective Service System Registration Certificate.'" Maggie looked at June. "This is Scott Twisdem's draft card." Maggie squinted to decipher the faded typed letters and numbers. "'Selective Service number blah, blah, blah. Born November 18, 1951, in Somerset Harbor, Maine. Brown eyes. Brown hair. Height six feet one inch, weight one sixty-eight.'" She looked at the birth date again, a strange sadness washing over her.

She handed Scott Twisdem's draft card to June and studied the other paper. "This one is for Will Rackelman. Similar information. Born September 14, 1951. He is described as five feet eleven inches tall with blond hair and blue eyes." She gave Will's card to June. "He was two months older than Scott."

June's brow furrowed. "I wonder why Will's draft card was hidden at the Twisdem Mansion. Why didn't he have it with him when he disappeared? Weren't young men required to keep it with them at all times?"

Maggie shrugged. "For that matter, why wasn't Scott's card in the car with him when it burned?"

"Maybe refusing to carry the cards was another way the boys protested the war." June placed the cards on top of the sideboard. "What else is in the hidden drawer?"

Maggie stuck her hand in the hiding place and fished out a heavy gold ring. She held it up between her right index finger and thumb. At first glance, she thought it was an ornate gold signet ring, but the flat top sported an engraved growling bear instead of initials. The bear was encircled by a garland of letters spelling *Somerset High School*, and it was flanked by *19* on one side and *70* on the other. Maggie rotated the ring and looked inside and found engraved initials. "'S.T.'"

"Scott Twisdem's high school ring." Maggie remembered Cynthia Moorman's story of their breakup. "I wonder if he put the ring back on after Cynthia broke up with him, or if he just hid it in that drawer."

June took the ring and placed it on the palm of one hand. "Does anyone ever wear high school rings after they graduate?"

Maggie thought of her own high school ring safely stashed in the back of her jewelry box. "I haven't worn mine in twenty-five years."

June put the ring on the sideboard next to the draft cards. "What else is in there?"

"This piece of paper." Maggie lifted a sheet of notebook paper from its hiding spot. "It looks like a poem." She lifted the paper closer so she could see the faded writing and read the four-stanza poem aloud:

> *I love you*
> *But you told me good-bye—*
> *One died, one cried, we tried, one big divide.*
> *Will we survive?*

> *Must I prove*
> *My worth to the world now?*
> *It's not my fight, but is war ever right?*
> *Must we kill?*
> *What are they—*
> *This duty and honor?*

Do you get to define both yours and mine?
I think not.

Tell me now
Who am I to love more—
My country, my family, my girl, my life?
You're killing me.

"Love, war, duty, honor," June said when Maggie stopped reading. "Passionate words."

"Yes, but look at this." Maggie held the paper up. "Beneath the poem. Do those look like bloody fingerprints to you?"

June took the paper and peered closely at the marks. "Sure could be, although I suppose it might be finger paint." She sighed, then returned the poem, ring, and draft cards to their hiding place and locked the drawer. "Maybe we'll find out more information at the historical society meeting tomorrow. And everyone will probably want to know what we've found out about the Twisdems, now that the auction has us all intrigued."

"Too bad I haven't found much."

"I'm sure they'll love to hear whatever we can tell them." June walked to the counter where she kept her purse. "I need to head home. I told Kurt I'd be home in time to fix dinner."

"No problem, I'll close up today," Maggie said.

"Thanks. And Kurt appreciates it too."

As June was putting on her coat, Maggie had one more thought. "The things hidden in the sideboard are by far the most personal items from the Twisdem Mansion," Maggie said. "Do you suppose the family would like them?"

June shrugged. "I have no idea. At this point, we don't even know if there's any family left."

9

"Oh come on, Maggie. It'll be fun. Please?" Daphne put her hands together like Emily had when she was a six-year-old begging for a snack before dinner.

Maggie searched for an answer. "We don't have a day spa in Somerset Harbor. There's a barber in town, but not a beauty salon. We'd have to drive to Pelican Cove."

"I would love that. It'd give us extra time to get to know each other."

Maggie had at least six items on her to-do list and didn't have time to spend on a day at the salon. Paperwork was stacked up in the office and the Twisdem antiques needed to be tagged and displayed in the shop. But Daphne's enthusiasm was infectious, and Maggie was pretty sure her future stepmother wouldn't take no for an answer. "I'd love to, as long as June doesn't need me in the shop and we can get a last-minute appointment." Maggie looked past Daphne to the unwashed dishes in the sink. "I'll call the salon after—"

"You go on and call now. Your father and I will clean the kitchen."

"Sure, I'll help," Neil said, strolling into the kitchen. "You two have your girls' morning out. I'll listen to the cool collection of records in the library."

"O-okay." Maggie was still getting accustomed to her father setting tables and washing dishes. And taking orders from his fiancée. As a retired bank executive, he was accustomed to being in charge. "I'll call from the office."

Leaving her father and Daphne laughing at the kitchen sink, Maggie sought a moment of solitude in the office. She sank into the desk chair to collect her thoughts. Everything was happening so fast. What else would Maggie discover?

First she called June, who told her to go on and enjoy her time with Daphne. Next, Maggie dialed Heather Taber, hairdresser and owner of Sea Salt Salon and Day Spa in Pelican Cove. Maggie begged for an emergency appointment for two.

"You're in luck. Mrs. Michaels and her sister called five minutes ago and cancelled their mani-pedi appointments," Heather said. "Can you be here in an hour?"

"Absolutely." Maggie hung up the phone and took a deep breath, then realized that she had completely forgotten to tell Emily about the wedding. Since Emily was likely studying, she sent a text: *Any chance of a visit to Somerset Harbor on Valentine's Day? Wedding day for your grandfather.*

Her phone rang thirty seconds later, and she answered it to hear her daughter exclaim, *"What?"*

"I didn't expect you to be free at the moment," Maggie replied, glad she wasn't the only one who was having difficulty wrapping her mind around the idea.

"I ducked out of study group. I just had to hear about this. Tell me everything, Mom."

· · · · · · · · · · · · · · · · ·

Maggie relaxed into the massage chair and listened as Daphne explained to Amber, the nail technician, why this day of beauty was so important.

"Maggie's father and I are getting married in a week." Daphne beamed. "I wanted to do some prewedding bonding with her."

Amber, a wisp of a young woman with bright pink streaks in her jet-black hair, looked at her client with curiosity. "That's pretty wicked," she said. "To find love at your age."

Maggie stifled a chuckle and looked at Daphne, who didn't

seem the least bit offended. "I know," she said, her eyes bright. "I certainly didn't expect it! Maggie's father took me completely by surprise."

Amber checked the temperature of Daphne's footbath and returned to massaging lotion into her client's hands. "What kind of wedding do you want?"

Maggie was thankful her own nail tech, Grace, was less talkative. She wanted to hear Daphne's response. What exactly did Daphne expect with little more than a week's notice?

"If we had more time, I'd love a glamorous wedding. Lots of flowers, twinkling lights, silk and tulle. Just like in the movies."

A smile tugged at Maggie's lips. *Ah, Daphne the farmer is an incurable romantic with a love of old Hollywood.* "Actually, a movie star was married at Sedgwick Manor back in the 1960s. Her name was—"

"Sylvia Sterling. Neil told me about it because he knows I'm a fan of old movies," Daphne said with stars in her eyes. "I love her films. Her heroines were always feisty, smart, and gorgeous. And she always got her man."

Maggie wished she'd paid more attention when her mother and Aunt Evelyn waxed poetic about the stunning starlet who'd brought Hollywood to Somerset Harbor. Maggie had never been one for glitz and glamour. "I'm afraid I don't know much about her."

"Well, she's not just a famous actress. Sylvia is a do-gooder. She started an education foundation for children who lacked money for college, and an organization that trains and provides therapy animals for people with physical and emotional disabilities. Isn't that neat?"

"It is," Maggie replied, although she was unsure whether the question was directed toward her or Amber.

"It's important to give back when you've been so blessed, don't you think?" Daphne paused as Amber began working on her other hand. "The time I spend teaching art to people with special needs is my favorite part of the week. My students are so appreciative."

Maggie felt the stress of the last few days melt away as her chair kneaded her back and Grace massaged her feet. Or perhaps the sense of peace came from releasing her anxiety about her father's surprise fiancée.

Maggie watched as Daphne's eyes fluttered closed when Amber began rubbing lotion on her feet. Daphne was an attractive woman. Her face had aged gracefully and was enhanced with minimal makeup. Like her wardrobe, her short hair was stylish but simple. Best of all, Maggie was now sure she had a good heart. Daphne loved Maggie's father and he loved her in return.

"She looks peaceful, doesn't she?" Grace broke her silence.

Maggie nodded, remembering the delight she had seen on her father's face as he helped Daphne wash the breakfast dishes. Her dad had his own life and Maggie wanted him to be happy, even if his joy was far away on a Michigan farm.

Daphne opened her eyes when Amber started placing spacers between her toes. "I think I dozed off a bit," she said, blinking.

"No wonder. You've been on the go nonstop since you arrived in Somerset Harbor." Maggie smiled. "Rest is good. You'll need all of your energy to plan your romantic wedding."

Maura O'Brien, the town's librarian, came and sat in the stylist's booth across from Daphne. Maggie caught Maura's eye and waved. "How are things at the library?"

"Quite well, Maggie. How are you?"

"Busy. Maura, meet my dad's fiancée, Daphne Bergman. We're having their wedding at Sedgwick Manor on Valentine's Day."

"Congratulations." Maura held an inch-long lock of her hair up to show Heather where to cut it. "Good luck with the wedding plans."

Daphne and Maggie spent the last part of their pedicures sharing pastimes. Maggie explained her love of needlecraft and reading, as well as how she had discovered her inadvertent talent for solving mysteries. Daphne described her beekeeping hobby and her passion for trail riding on horseback.

As Maggie and Daphne got ready to leave, Maura and Heather were discussing the Twisdem family and the auction. Stalling to eavesdrop, Maggie rummaged around in her purse, feigning a search for her wallet.

"Such a sad story," Heather said, combing out Maura's hair.

"After all these years, nobody really knows what caused the wreck. You know, I heard Marilyn Twisdem, bless her soul, had a few coherent moments right after the accident and she told a nurse that Scott's friend was in the car when it crashed."

Maggie's ears pricked up. What she wouldn't give to know exactly what Marilyn had said.

Daphne tugged on Maggie's arm. "You don't need your wallet. This is my treat."

"Thank you," Maggie stammered, then reluctantly let Daphne lead her to the front counter and away from any further Twisdem gossip.

. . . .

After dinner, Maggie left her father and Daphne at home with a sink full of dinner dishes to wash and more records to listen to. On her way to the historical society meeting, she dialed James's phone number.

"Evening, Maggie. To what do I owe this honor?"

She smiled. "I have a favor to ask."

"I'll do anything I can for you."

She gave him a quick rundown of the week's events, including her father's surprise fiancée and impending wedding. "I'd like to do something special for them. Dad loves Cole Loveren's music and I want to treat them to the concert. Do you know anyone who could score last-minute tickets?"

"At your service," James said. "I can make a few calls. I'll give you a buzz as soon as I have news."

"One more thing." Maggie eased into a parking space near the teal Victorian that housed the historical society. "Do you know anything about the Rackelman family? Will Rackelman was a friend of Scott Twisdem. Evidently, he disappeared after the Twisdem wreck. Do you know if anyone has heard from him over the years?"

"The family still lives in Somerset Harbor, but I'm not sure where. I'll ask around and let you know."

"Thanks. You're really Mr. Helpful today. Coffee is on me the next time I see you in The Busy Bean."

James laughed. "I'll do my best to earn it."

. . . .

Maggie was pleased to see Ina Linton already sitting at the table when she walked into the meeting. "Ina, how are you feeling? We missed you at the last meeting."

"I'm fit as a fiddle. You know nothing keeps me down very long." She gestured for Maggie to sit in the seat beside her. "I heard the call for the attempted burglary at Carriage House Antiques on the police scanner. Did they catch the guy?"

Ina didn't miss any newsworthy events in Somerset Harbor. She also knew more about the town's residents than anyone, and Maggie wanted to ask her about the Twisdem family.

"Not yet, but I'm hopeful," Maggie said as Ruth walked in with a carafe of water and filled the coffee maker before taking her seat at the head of the table. "Life has been strange since the Twisdem auction. I've been trying to find out more about the family."

Liz, Fran, and June joined them at the table, exchanging greetings as they took their seats.

"Maggie, I got all of the Twisdem items priced before I closed up the shop," June said. "All of the box lot merchandise is out on the floor, but we'll need some help getting the furniture on display. That tiger maple sideboard is hefty. I'll call the movers tomorrow."

"Sounds good." Maggie returned her attention to Ina. "I'm gathering information about the Twisdem family. Can you tell me anything about them?"

"Well, the family isn't what it once was, that's for sure. Back in the day, they were active in the town. That all changed in 1970 when—"

Ina's words were lost in the air as Daisy breezed into the room, a tray of cookies in one hand and her car keys in the other. "I understand there's to be a wedding at Sedgwick Manor," she announced, looking at Maggie. "Why did I find out about it from Maura O'Brien as I served her chicken salad croissant, instead of hearing it from my friend?"

"Well, um, I've been a bit preoccupied lately." Maggie stumbled over her words as mouths dropped around the table.

"You've been holding out on us, Maggie," Ina piped up. "Who's the lucky fellow?"

All eyes turned toward Maggie.

"Oh, I'm not getting married. My father is. In a week."

Maggie brought the group up to speed, explaining her father's strange phone calls, his last-minute visit, and his arrival with Daphne. "Yesterday, they walked into the foyer and out of the blue asked me if the wedding could be held at Sedgwick Manor. I'm a little overwhelmed, to tell you the truth."

"That's huge news," Fran said in her soft voice.

Maggie looked at the women around her. "I want to give Dad and Daphne a beautiful wedding—even though they said they don't need anything fancy—but I don't know where to start."

Liz frowned. "It's awfully little time to plan a wedding."

Daisy slid the cookie tray into the center of the table and sat next to Maggie. "Dig in, everyone. It looks like we have a wedding to prepare. And luckily, I have a plan."

Ina grabbed a cookie and a napkin. "Let's hear it."

"First, we need a theme. When I was serving Maura's lunch, she said Daphne mentioned Sylvia Sterling's wedding with stars in her eyes," Daisy said. "So I was thinking: Wouldn't it be fun to use the Sterling wedding as the inspiration?"

Ina clapped her hands with glee. "I remember that wedding. It was the event of the season in Somerset Harbor and Hollywood. The papers covered it for a week."

Ruth held up a manila envelope. "Daisy called me this afternoon and asked if the historical society had any photos of the Sterling wedding, which of course we do." She spread several black-and-white photos across the table. "Maggie, if you agree, Daisy and I thought we could study the photos and divide up the planning duties."

"I'm more than agreeable. I'm grateful for your help."

Liz picked up a photo of the bride wearing a tea-length wedding dress with three-quarter sleeves and a lace bodice, which she'd accessorized with gloves and a birdcage veil. "Sylvia Sterling may have been glamorous, but she was also classy."

"Daphne is well over six feet tall," Maggie said, gazing at the photo in Liz's hand. "Finding a dress on short notice may be a challenge."

Liz clucked reassuringly. "Don't you worry. I've helped with dozens of weddings at the church over the years. I know the best places to look."

The women spent the next twenty minutes brainstorming ideas, creating a to-do list, and assigning volunteers.

"Ladies, we do not have a lot of time, so we best get to work." Ruth passed a stack of papers around the table. "Here are copies of the *Herald's* coverage of the wedding. Use this as a guide. Let's meet back here tomorrow night. Will that work for everyone?"

All enthusiastically agreed.

Maggie's face flushed with appreciation for her friends. "Thank you. I have no idea how I would've pulled this off without you."

As Maggie stood, Daisy wrapped her in a hug. "Rest easy, Maggie. That's what friends are for."

Maggie hurried along the path from the shop to the house, her gloved hand grasping a plastic bag containing the hand-written poem and draft cards from the sideboard. After a pro-ductive morning getting the Twisdem furniture arranged on the sales floor, she was looking forward to sharing news about the wedding plans and the hidden treasure with her father and Daphne. She heard their voices before she opened the door.

"All we need is a minister and Maggie." Neil's voice was soothing. "You're making this more complicated than it needs be. Just calm down."

"Don't tell me to calm down like I'm a child." Daphne's angry words made Maggie hesitate to open the door. "I want a real wedding with flowers, music, and a wedding dress. My first wedding was three minutes in front of the justice of the peace."

"We have less than a week." Her father always was the voice of reason.

Maggie took a deep breath, opened the door, and strolled into the kitchen. "Hi. I'm sorry I ducked out before breakfast. June needed help with the new displays." She looked from her dad to Daphne. "Everything all right?"

"We're fine," her dad replied.

"We are *not*," Daphne said, hands on her hips. "We disagree on the wedding plans. He wants easy and unimaginative. I don't need a big to-do, but I'd like it to be special."

Although it was nearly eleven o'clock, their breakfast dishes remained on the table. The spat had apparently been going on awhile.

Maggie held up her hands. "I have news that might change things. I was going to tell you last night, but you'd already gone upstairs. Please, sit down." She herded them to the breakfast table and placed the plastic bag on a clean spot. "We can have a beautiful wedding here at the manor, the kind Daphne wants. And we can be ready for a Valentine's Day ceremony." She looked from one shocked face to the other. "Do you trust me?"

"Yes," they responded in unison.

"But how?" Ever the pragmatist, Neil looked dubious.

"My friends at the historical society heard about the wedding, and they want to plan the entire event. They're a creative bunch. Ideas were zinging around at our meeting last night."

Daphne jumped out of her chair and threw her arms around Maggie's neck. "How will we ever thank you?"

"Be happy, for starters." She returned Daphne's embrace warmly.

When Daphne had sat back down, Maggie removed the ring, draft cards, and poem from the bag and spread them on the table. "Not to change the subject, but I'd love it if you could provide me with some insight into Vietnam War history. June and I found these in a hidden drawer of a sideboard from the Twisdem Mansion. One of the draft cards belonged to Scott Twisdem, as did the ring, I think. He was killed in a car wreck in 1970. The second draft card was for his friend, Will Rackelman, although I have no idea why it was in a piece of the Twisdems' furniture."

Neil picked up the draft cards and studied both sides. "Boy, do these bring back memories. I was terrified my number would come up. I knew the right thing to do was to serve if my country needed me, but the thought of being in a war zone terrified me." He dropped the cards onto the table. "I feel lucky I had a high draft number. I carried my card for a long time, but I don't know what happened to it since."

"What a beautiful class ring," Daphne said. "Do you know anything about the fella it belonged to?"

"Not much, but I'm working on it." Maggie picked up the ring and pointed to the initials. "This must have been Scott's. His girlfriend had broken up with him and returned the ring a few weeks before he died. I met her and she definitely has regrets. It's sad."

"What's this?" Her father unfolded the paper with the poem on it. He read it, mumbling the words to himself.

Maggie shrugged. "It's a poem I found with the ring and draft cards. I don't know if Scott, Will, or someone else wrote it."

He read the four stanzas again and frowned. "Sounds familiar, but I can't place it. That's what happens when you reach my age."

"Oh, stop with that 'my age' stuff," Daphne said, playfully swatting him on the arm. "We're still spring chickens with a lot of life left."

"Amen to that." Maggie laughed just as her cell phone rang. "I need to take this in the office." They nodded, and she left the kitchen. "Hi, James," she said, walking to the office. "Any luck?"

"Good morning to you too," he said, chuckling. "And yes on both counts. I can give you the tickets this afternoon when I pick you up to go visit Will Rackelman's sister and brother. If you have time, that is."

She sat at her desk and looked at her to-do list. "I'll make time. When?"

"I told Ron Rackelman we would be there between one and two o'clock."

"I'll be ready by one. Thank you, James, both for locating the Rackelmans and getting the tickets. I owe you one. Or two, technically."

As soon as she finished talking with James, Maggie received a text message from Liz. *Ina and I can pick up Daphne for wedding dress shopping in 30 minutes. Is she free?*

. . . .

"Here you go, four tickets to the Cole Loveren concert." James extended an envelope to Maggie as soon as they were seated in his black Mercedes.

"Four?"

"I'd like to hear Cole Loveren, and it might be interesting to double-date with your dad and Daphne."

Did he say "double-date"? Maggie nodded. "Sounds like fun." She pulled a roll of clipped bills from her purse and offered it to James. "Dad will go nuts when he sees them."

"Let this one be on me, Maggie."

Maggie looked out the window and chose her words carefully. "I'm grateful, but I can't. I need to do this for my father so he will know I support his marriage."

"I understand," James said, accepting the money. "You're a good person, Maggie."

Her cheeks tingled, a sure sign she was blushing. "Takes one to know one."

James smiled as he started the car and pulled out of the driveway. "We're going to Ron Rackelman's house. He lives a few blocks from the old family home. His younger sister, Gloria, will be there too."

"Did you have a hard time finding them?"

"Not at all. I found Ron through the high school alumni association. He contacted his sister." He braked for a stop sign and paused to look at Maggie. "What do you hope to learn from them, anyway?"

"I'm not sure. Everything connected with the items from the Twisdem Mansion seems so sad. I'm just compelled to know more about those young men who died too soon. Scott, Will, and Philip would be about my father's age now."

A few minutes later, they turned onto a lane lined with

clapboard cottages and tall evergreen trees. Ron Rackelman's place was charming. To the left of the front door, an American flag waved in the slight breeze. Maggie's heart beat faster as they walked the stone pathway to the house. *Can Ron and his sister help me decipher the poem from the sideboard?*

The door opened as James lifted his fist to knock.

"You must be Alderman Bennett. I'm Ron Rackelman." Ron opened the door a little wider.

"Great to meet you," James said as the men clasped hands. "Call me James. This is Maggie Watson, the antiques dealer I mentioned on the phone."

"Thank you for seeing us." Maggie also shook Ron's hand.

"Gloria and I are always happy to talk about our brother. It helps us remember. Please come in." He stepped back to let them pass.

Ron waved Maggie and James into the foyer and led them into a living room furnished with an eclectic array of antiques and newer furnishings. "Have a seat. Gloria will be out in a second." He gestured to a gray leather sofa before sitting in one of two matching striped chairs. An array of photo albums was spread across the coffee table. "Her daughter called right before you arrived."

"Here I am." Gloria glided into the room and exchanged introductions with James and Maggie before sitting beside her brother.

Ron and Gloria looked like bookends with matching gray hair, slightly lined faces, and deep blue eyes. *Does Will, wherever he is, look like his siblings?* Maggie pulled the plastic bag out of her purse, removed Will's draft card, and handed it to Gloria. "I found this tucked inside a secret drawer in a sideboard purchased at the Twisdem Mansion auction. It was with Scott's draft card and a couple other things. I thought you might like to see it."

Will's sister stared at the card until her eyes filled with tears. She ran her fingers over his signature, scribbles made by a teenage boy nearly five decades earlier. "Other girls lost brothers in Vietnam, and the majority of them at least know where and when they died." She gave the draft card to Ron. "We don't even have that. No funeral. No closure."

Maggie's heart hurt for Will's siblings. "What do you remember about Will and Scott Twisdem?"

Ron and Gloria exchanged a long glance. The air in the room was heavy. After several seconds, Ron finally spoke. "They were buddies from grade school into high school, until Scott fell for Cynthia and began spending all of his time with her." Ron rubbed his eyes. "They remained friends, but as Scott became more serious with Cynthia, Will developed a friendship with Philip Johns. Philip taught Will to play the guitar, and he was pretty good too."

Gloria leaned forward and gazed out the picture window. "Will looked up to Philip. He was a very talented guitar player, and he allowed Will to hang out with his band. It gave Will self-confidence when he put a guitar in his hand."

Maggie wasn't sure if talking about Will was therapeutic for Gloria or not.

James cleared his throat. "What happened when Philip enlisted and went to Vietnam?"

"Will was shaken as anyone would be, but he honestly believed Philip would return home and they'd re-form the band." Gloria leafed through a photo album and pointed out a picture of Will and Philip with guitars in hand. "Philip's death affected Will. He became obsessed with antiwar demonstrations and participated in protests on college campuses. He handed out flyers urging people to protest the war and men to flee to Canada."

Ron shook his head with regret. "Ironically, he began coming home with black eyes and bruises as the peaceful demonstrations turned into riots and became more and more violent. He became so active in protests, I think he was put on some sort of watch list."

Maggie remembered Cynthia's comments about Scott and Will. "How did protesting affect his friendships?"

"By the time he disappeared, Will had alienated most of his friends. He was so passionate about what he was doing." Gloria pulled a tissue from the box on the table next to her. "After Scott's girlfriend broke up with him, though, he and Will began hanging out again."

James sat on the end of his seat, clearly engrossed in the story. He looked at Gloria. "When did you last see Will?"

"The day before the Twisdems' car crash. We were all stunned when Will's number came up so early in the draft lottery. Mom and Dad wanted to take all of us to see family friends in Vermont for a long weekend since we all knew it was just a matter of time before he got a letter. My dad and Will got into a shouting match because Will refused to go with us. He was talking of going to Canada to dodge the draft. It ended when Dad gave in and ordered the rest of us to go to the car." Gloria bit her lip. "My last memory of Will was as we were walking out the door. He hugged me and said, 'I love you, little sister,' and closed the door behind me. Mom and Dad thought he'd never leave home. But I knew he wouldn't be here when we came back."

Ron closed his eyes and took a deep breath. "When we returned from our trip that Monday, Will was gone, along with his savings, clothes, and guitar. We never heard from him again."

"Do you think Will disappeared before or after Scott was killed in the accident?" James asked the question that was nagging Maggie.

Ron shrugged. "We have no way of knowing exactly when he left. Why would it matter?"

"I don't know." James held his hands open in supposition. "Maybe he left because his two best friends were now gone and he wanted to escape the memories."

"I guess it's possible." Gloria dabbed her eyes with a tissue. "I'm sorry for the tears. After almost fifty years, you'd think I could talk about Will without crying."

"I have one more thing to show you." Maggie pulled the poem from the plastic bag and handed it to Ron. "Do you recognize this poem? I found it with the ring and draft cards."

He read the verses aloud. "I can't say I do. But this is Will's handwriting."

"I don't recognize it either," Gloria said. "Will was always jotting things down. Descriptions of people, jokes, words of wisdom."

"Even at a young age, Will had a way with words and an interest in people." Ron's voice was husky. His eyes filled with tears too. He shook his head. "I'm sorry."

They've had enough. Maggie replaced the items in the bag and stood. "We've taken too much of your time. I apologize for bringing up difficult memories, but I appreciate you telling your stories. I'd like to keep these a little longer, if you don't mind, but I'll get them back to you soon."

"Oh, please don't apologize." Gloria stood up and hugged her. "People have always been afraid to talk about Will. It was nice to share memories, despite the tears. You keep Will's things as long as you need to."

Maggie and James said their good-byes and promised to let the siblings know if they unearthed any information about their brother's disappearance.

"Well, that was intense," James said as they walked down the path to the car.

Sadness settled over Maggie like a fog. "I feel so bad for them." A bright red cardinal launched itself from the mailbox and Maggie followed its flight path as it soared into a leafless tree next door. "What a beautiful—"

A movement by the tree caught her eye. Maggie slowed her steps and put her hand on James's arm. "Do you see that man with the fedora lurking in the trees? I've been seeing him a lot since the Twisdem auction," she whispered. "I think he followed us here."

As James swiveled his head toward the trees, Fedora Man turned and ran.

"People don't run away for no reason," James said before sprinting toward the trees.

Stunned, Maggie watched the two men disappear behind the house next door. Shaking off her fear, she grabbed the pepper spray from her bag and jogged after them.

She dashed to the house and crept along the side wall until she reached the backyard. Inching into the yard, Maggie looked for signs of the two men, but all was quiet. A wall of logs taller than Maggie was stacked a few feet away from a fire pit surrounded by four Adirondack chairs. The cardinal and his mate perched nonchalantly on an empty birdbath on the other side of the pit. A clump of evergreens gathered at the back of the lawn.

Where did they go? The cardinals took flight from the birdbath, their haunting metallic chirp sounding like a warning as they flew to the top of the tallest evergreen. Maggie's heart beat faster. Twigs snapped and Fedora Man emerged from behind the woodpile at full speed, running toward the stand of trees.

Maggie started to chase after him, but as she was passing behind the woodpile, she came across James kneeling on the ground, mud covering his arms and torso.

"James! Are you okay?" Maggie hurried to his side.

"I'm fine. Probably shouldn't wear wingtips the next time I plan to chase somebody through the mud, though."

Maggie helped him to his feet, then gazed toward the grove of trees. Fedora Man had vanished as though he'd never been there.

11

Fifteen minutes later, Maggie waved good-bye to James from the front door of Sedgwick Manor. She imagined he couldn't wait to get home for a shower after his messy fall. As she walked into the house, she heard laughter filtering from the library. She crossed the foyer to find Daphne doing a fine imitation of a model's runway walk in a white tea-length wedding dress and matching pumps. Maggie's father and Ina sat in the chairs, clapping. Liz, playing wedding coordinator, was standing to the side, watching.

When the clapping stopped and Daphne posed for Liz to snap a photo on her phone, Maggie stepped into the room. "Wow, you have a dress already?"

Daphne spun around again, looking like a much younger woman. "Isn't it beautiful? My new best friends, Liz and Ina, found it for me."

"It's stunning." Maggie turned to her friends. "How in the world did you score a vintage dress in the right size so quickly?"

"Cooperative effort," Ina said. "Liz surfed the Internet and located every thrift store between here and Portland. I called each one to see if they had a vintage wedding dress for a statuesque lady. We found five, so we picked up Daphne and took a road trip."

"None of the first four fit, of course," Liz said. "But the fifth one was the charm."

Daphne stooped to remove her heels. "It's perfect."

June tapped on the library door. "Maggie, I wanted to give you these receipts—" She walked in and stopped short. "Oh, hi, everyone. Sorry, I didn't realize you were busy."

"No problem at all. June, I'd like to introduce my dad, Neil Segal." Maggie gestured toward her father, then waved a hand toward Daphne. "And this is his fiancée, Daphne. She's just showing us this gorgeous bridal dress Liz and Ina found for her."

June's jaw dropped. "Isn't it bad luck for the groom to see the bride's dress before the wedding?"

Daphne's hand flew to her mouth in horror. "How could I forget?" She ran to the window and pulled the drapes around her. "Neil, leave the library. Now!"

Maggie froze, unsure of how to respond. She didn't believe in bad luck. Her father shifted in his chair. *Should she go to her father or Daphne?* She was grateful when Liz put her arm around Daphne and gently removed the curtain from her hands.

"Daphne, I think God will bless your marriage whether or not your groom sees the wedding dress before the ceremony," Liz said, guiding the older woman away from the window. "Neil can stay where he is. Everything will be all right."

Daphne's face relaxed. "It's just an old wives' tale, right?"

"I'm so sorry. It was a gut reaction and a silly old saying." June blushed deeply.

"It's fine, June," Maggie said. "No harm done. Come on in and join us."

June handed a fistful of receipts to Maggie. "I dashed over to tell you that word's circulated about the Twisdem pieces. We're having a banner afternoon, and that's just the items from the box lot so far. After the last batch of customers left, I couldn't wait to tell you the news."

Maggie flipped through the papers with her thumb. "This is incredible. Do you need my help?"

"Everything is under control, but I'd better get back." June put a hand on Daphne's shoulder. "Your dress is beautiful. Please forget what I said."

Daphne smoothed the skirt of her dress and nodded. "It's already forgotten."

As June turned to go, Maggie thought of something and caught her arm. "Just a second." She retrieved the bag with the draft cards, Scott's class ring, and the poem and handed it to June. "I don't want these just floating around with all the strange things going on. Will you put them back where we found them? We'll just need to remember to take them back out if the sideboard sells."

"You got it." June gave her a hug and left.

Ina piped up. "Liz, we've fulfilled our wedding dress promise, and it's time for us to go too. If I know Maggie, she has a long list of things to do before tonight's wedding planning session."

"You do know me well," Maggie said with a smile. She would be glad to have time alone with her father and Daphne so she could give them the concert tickets.

Maggie walked Ina and Liz to the front entrance and hugged each of them. "I don't know how you worked the miracle of finding a dress so fast, but it's gorgeous. Thank you."

Ina waved her off. "Don't be silly, Maggie. No need to thank us."

Liz smiled and said, "God helps those who help themselves."

When she closed the door behind the women, Maggie leaned back against it. *What on earth would I do without my friends?*

As she returned to the library, the sounds of Creedence Clearwater Revival's "Fortunate Son" filled the air. Her dad never went long without turning on music. "I have a surprise for you," Maggie said, grabbing her purse from the table where she'd dropped it earlier. She pulled out the concert tickets and held them out to her father. "Tickets to see Cole Loveren tomorrow night with me and my friend James. It's an engagement gift."

Neil took the tickets from Maggie and stared at them. When he lifted his head, his face was filled with emotion. "I haven't seen him in concert in thirty years." He drew his daughter and his future bride to him in a group hug. "And now I get to experience Cole Loveren live with my two favorite people in the world."

"You are an angel," Daphne whispered to Maggie.

"It's my pleasure, really," Maggie said.

As they broke off the embrace, Daphne stifled a yawn. "The shopping and fashion show are getting to me. I'm heading upstairs to take a short nap."

Maggie checked her watch. It was four o'clock. She had plenty of time to do some research before the wedding planning meeting at the historical society. "I think I'll go to the library and see what I can dig up about what happened here during the height of the war."

"I'd like to go with you if you don't mind," Neil said.

Maggie smiled. "Not at all. It'll be nice to spend some time with you."

Neil kissed Daphne's cheek. "Later, honey."

Daphne returned the kiss in kind. "Happy researching. See you two after my nap."

. . . .

"Cool building," Neil said as they crossed Broad Street from the public parking lot to the library, a two-story building that resembled the hull of a dry-docked boat. "Porthole-style windows to boot."

Maggie chuckled. "There's no shortage of boat homages in Somerset Harbor. We're very proud of our shipping history."

"I see," he said, holding the door open for her. "Get it? Sea?" He jerked a thumb in the direction of the ocean.

Maggie rolled her eyes good-naturedly at her dad's amused quip. "That was awful, Dad. Maura, the librarian, maintains a section of books dedicated to local family genealogy, businesses, organizations, and famous current or former residents." She pointed toward the area behind the word *Reference* painted in blue on the back wall. "In fact, we're headed that way."

"Hello, Maggie." Maura waved in greeting as Maggie and her father walked by the library circulation desk. "Did you and your father's fiancée enjoy your manicures?"

"We did." Maggie put her hand on Neil's arm. "This is my father, Neil Segal. Dad, this is our town librarian, Maura O'Brien. Daphne met her at the salon."

"Ms. O'Brien, nice to meet you." He smiled. "I see you run a tight ship."

Maura's green eyes twinkled. "Aye, we do, and you should be here on Talk Like a Pirate Day, matey." She waved to a couple of teenage girls on their way to the young adult section, then refocused on Maggie. "Anything I can help you with today?"

"We're looking for information about Vietnam War protests held in or near Somerset Harbor," Maggie said. "Can you send us in the right direction?"

Maura cocked her head. "Interesting topic. I have the perfect book for you. Follow me." She came out from behind the counter and led them to a cart of books near the reference desk. "Our high school juniors have a term paper to write about local history. They're assigned to choose an event or person and explain its importance to Somerset Harbor and beyond. I pulled these books for them."

She ran her right index finger along the book spines until she found a slender blue hardback. "*Lost Innocence: Somerset Harbor and the Vietnam War* was written by the late local historian Douglass Turner in 1976, ten years after his son was killed in Vietnam. He interviewed families who lost sons, young men who made it home, and others relieved to have missed the draft." Maura handed the book to Maggie. "People are surprised to learn we had a peaceful demonstration in Somerset Harbor in 1968 after a popular musician was killed."

"Philip Johns?"

"That's him. You can read all about it in the book, so I'll leave you to it."

The tome was light and thin, and Maggie was doubtful they'd find much enlightening information inside. "Thanks, Maura."

"Anytime. Let me know if I can help." The librarian returned to her station behind the checkout desk.

Maggie led her father to a small table tucked in the back corner of the reference section. "We can start with this book and see what we find." She eyed the clock hanging over the reference desk. "We have about ninety minutes until the historical society meeting starts."

"Let's get to it, then." Neil pulled a chair out for his daughter and sat in the one next to her.

Maggie grabbed her notepad and pen from her purse. She opened the book and turned to the dedication page. "'In memory of my courageous son, Airman Wesley Turner, who gave his life for his country on April 3, 1966, when his plane was shot down over North Vietnam,'" she read aloud. Sadness washed over her. "I can't imagine how much inner strength it must have taken for Douglass Turner to research and write this book after losing his son."

Maggie and her father stared at the photo of the stern, handsome young airman in uniform.

"People handle grief in different ways, Maggie." Neil turned the page past the acknowledgements to the table of contents. "Fight or flight. Some face the loss head-on with a project to help them make sense of it, while others run away in order to stop trying to make an altered life resume as usual."

Maggie raised her head to look in his eyes, to ask an unspoken question. *Is that why you moved to Michigan after Mom died?* The answer was clear in his expression. At that moment, the hurt she'd nursed since her mother's death began to heal. "I can understand that."

Maggie pulled her gaze from her father's face and scanned the table of contents. Chapter titles included "Legacy of Heroes: Pre-Vietnam War Losses," "A Brief History of the Vietnam War," "Local Reaction," and "Hometown Heroes." She opened to the section about local demonstrations.

The first passage recounted students gathering for prayer and a moment of silence in memory of the author's son on May 10, 1966. The memorial was led by Wesley Turner's younger brother, Matthew, a sophomore at the school.

The chapter continued with a description of a peaceful group of students lined up just outside of the high school property. The accompanying photo showed a dozen or so students with heads apparently bowed in prayer. The caption read: *Upon learning their former classmate Philip Johns, class of 1968, had been killed in Vietnam, a large group of students led by senior Will Rackelman reacted somberly to the news.*

Comments from Somerset Harbor High School students and faculty were included. A few words from Reverend Blaine Weatherall, minister of Old Faith Chapel at the time, closed the section.

On the bottom of the page, a photo of Will distributing antiwar flyers along Shoreline Drive was accompanied by quotes from several residents, some of them supporting Will's action, but several questioning the teen's patriotism. The author didn't interject an opinion.

Maggie turned the page.

"Here's a close-up of Will Rackelman and Scott Twisdem." Maggie looked at the two teens holding a sign with *End the war in Vietnam NOW!* painted in big, bold letters. Scott's dark hair was neatly trimmed above brooding eyes laced with emotion, perhaps fear. Will's face was contorted into a sneer, his longer blond hair tangling in the breeze.

Neil studied the photo cutline. "Those boys weren't playing. This must have been some protest. That's a battalion of police behind them."

She studied Scott Twisdem's face and stance. "Scott's facial expression and body language are so different from Will's."

Her father held the book closer. "I wonder what he was thinking. Do you suppose he was reacting to the atrocities of war or the activities he was pulled into?"

Maggie shook her head. "Beats me, but I'd give my eyeteeth to find out. Less than six months after this photo was taken, one boy was dead and the other missing. What did those boys get themselves into?"

12

The moon was hidden behind clouds when Maggie pulled into the parking lot a block away from the historical society. She'd circled around the building twice, but all of the street parking was taken. Normally, walking a block or two wasn't a big deal, but her day had been nonstop activity already and she was tired. However, she was still looking forward to spending the next hour or so hearing about the plans her friends were making for her father's Hollywood-worthy wedding.

She inhaled deeply and looked toward the dark street beyond the lights. Had she imagined the movement in the shadows? Her left hand on the door handle, Maggie dug into her purse with her right hand and pulled out her trusty pepper spray.

"You're getting yourself spooked, Maggie," she said to disturb the silence. "Snap out of it." She opened the car door, swept her eyes around the half-filled parking lot, and got out of the car. With the pink canister clutched in her right hand, Maggie walked at a fast clip toward the street.

She dashed across Water Way and ran down the sidewalk between patches of light from the lampposts. Footsteps fell in behind her about halfway to the historical society. After several paces, she gritted her teeth and whirled around to face her attacker, brandishing her pepper spray.

The street was empty, except for a black cat trotting across the road. Flustered, Maggie jogged the rest of the way to the building, giving thanks for her sensible shoes. Once inside, she lingered in the front room to catch her breath, returning the canister to her purse and running her fingers through her hair. She didn't want to explain how she allowed herself to get spooked by a stray cat.

Her mood took an upswing when she entered the meeting room. Not only was the air filled with the inviting aroma of warming food, but the table was covered with wedding paraphernalia, from silk flowers and tulle to a variety of glass containers. Bridal magazines and photo albums were open for inspection. *They did all this for my dad, and they don't even know him.*

"Wow, you've all been busy." Maggie pulled her attention away from the table and grinned. "How will I ever repay you?"

Liz put her arm around Maggie's shoulder. "You won't. Friends help friends when needed. It's what we do."

"Please keep your receipts so Dad and I can reimburse you." Her eyes welled with tears. "You are all so amazing to do this for us. Thank you."

"We'll discuss the money stuff later." Daisy began handing out small paper plates and forks. "Let's start with the important stuff, like the food tasting."

"I love the way this woman thinks," Ruth said, taking a plate from Daisy. "Tell us about the menu."

"Two little birdies—namely Liz and Ina—said that as they shopped for a wedding dress, Daphne mentioned having a morning wedding. So, I figured we should do a no-fuss but elegant brunch menu for ten to fifteen people. These are recipes I've fixed for lots of special events." She stepped to the left end of the serving table and lifted the lid off one of two chafing dishes. "Here we have two varieties of mini-quiche—sausage and cheese, and spinach and onion. For the wedding, I'll make quiche pies and cut them into wedges." She uncovered the second dish. "This is a divine spiced fruit my mother made at Christmas each year."

"It smells amazing, Daisy," Maggie said, sniffing the air appreciatively.

Daisy uncovered a tray hidden beneath a tea towel. "I've also brought a selection of breads to try. I often serve sweet bread with this quiche-fruit combination, but I wanted to give you all several different options to choose from. We have zucchini muffins, cinnamon scones, apple bread, and homemade herb-dusted potato bread."

Ruth plucked a pair of petite quiches from the serving dish and dropped them on her plate with tongs. "Let's nibble while we talk about the ceremony, flowers, and bridal dress. We can end our meeting with a vote on the food. Though how I'll pick a favorite, I have no idea."

When everyone was seated at the table with a full plate, conversation lagged a little as the ladies began tasting the food. Ina broke the silence.

"Wait, what about the wedding cake?" She turned to Daisy. "Do we have a wedding cake ordered?"

"Oh no!" Daisy cried. "I was so enthralled with the brunch menu, I forgot all about the cake."

Liz lifted her hand. "I think I can help. Clair Gregory is running a special for brides who order their wedding cakes between now and Valentine's Day." She rooted around in her purse and pulled out a small piece of paper clipped to a business card. "If anyone can make the perfect cake, it's Clair."

Maggie breathed a sigh of relief. Clair's parents, Nate and Opal, owned the landscaping and cleaning services that kept Sedgwick Manor in peak condition. They were also good friends of hers, and their daughter was a top-notch baker. "That's a great idea. Do you mind calling her?"

"Consider it done." Liz dabbed her mouth with a napkin. "Oh, and I've spoken with David and he's happy to do the ceremony. He put Valentine's Day on his calendar. Daphne and Neil will need to call the church and set a time to discuss the ceremony with him."

Liz pulled out her cell phone. "We have a bride's dress, thanks to Ina's love of thrift stores and one shopkeeper's willingness to make a few phone calls." She brought up a photo of Daphne modeling the dress. "Isn't it perfect?"

The photo elicited "oohs" and "aahs" from around the table as the phone was passed from friend to friend.

"All it took was calling twenty thrift stores and taking a road trip to Portland," Ina quipped. "It was fun, though, and we had a chance to get to know the bride. She's a hoot and very sweet."

Ruth set her empty plate aside. "That leaves the flowers. The photos we have from Sylvia Sterling's wedding showed lots of greenery, lilies of the valley, and miniature pink roses. We looked online and printed several photos to give you an idea of what Fran and I thought would work for decorations and the bridal bouquet."

"We're thinking simple and elegant," Fran said. "Sylvia had a garland of greens and roses running up the banister, which made a stunning visual. We'll add tulle to cut down on the amount of flowers and greenery. It'll be a less expensive adaptation."

Ruth reached for a long piece of faux greenery and demonstrated how the tulle could be draped around it as an accent. She added a sprig of lilies of the valley and a few roses. "It can be done with fresh or artificial flowers."

Maggie smiled. "Daphne will love it. If we have the ceremony in front of the window in the living room, the ocean view will provide most of the decoration we need."

"Our thoughts exactly." Ruth held up a photo of a cascade bouquet with miniature roses, lilies of the valley, and trailing greenery. "This bouquet is similar to Sylvia's. At first I thought we'd make it smaller, but I think if we make it full at the top with a long tapering tail, it may provide the floral impact we need for the room."

"That leads us to the dining room decorations." Fran nodded toward the collection of glass containers. "We thought three small flower arrangements would add color but not clutter the table. We can make bouquets using one rose, a sprig of lilies of the valley, and greenery."

Ina spread the photos in front of her and gazed at them. "This reminds me of the formal parties at the Twisdem Mansion back in the day. The whole house would be ablaze with candles and draped in floral garlands. It was quite grand."

"Everything the Twisdems did back then was large-scale grand." Ruth chuckled. "This will be a small-scale grand event."

Maggie was thoroughly pleased with the plans her friends had made. "I guess all we need now is a head count and a decision on whether to use silk or fresh flowers." Maggie checked off the items on the wedding to-do list and added a couple of tasks. "I'll talk to Daphne about the flowers and a guest list. I don't think they plan to send invitations, but I know they'd like all of you to attend. Of course, I'll call Emily with an update."

"I'd be honored to attend," Liz said, eliciting nods from the others. "What about your father's siblings and Daphne's children?"

"I thought of calling them, at least my aunt and uncles. I don't know how to reach Daphne's family." She remembered what her father and Daphne said about eloping to keep the peace in the family. "I'll start with Emily and go from there."

· · · · · · · · · · · · · · · · ·

Maggie was still pondering the guest list as the group locked up the building thirty minutes later. *Should we invite Dad's siblings and Daphne's children? Would they welcome that surprise? On the other hand, wouldn't it be worse if they found out Dad and Daphne got married and they didn't know anything about it?* She knew she would have to do some more thinking about it before coming to a decision.

The group dispersed. Fran and Ina stowed the decorations in Fran's car while Ruth helped Daisy load her dishes into her SUV.

"It's really dark out here," Liz said to Maggie as they walked down the stairs and looked toward Water Way. "Where are you parked?"

Remembering her experience walking to the meeting, Maggie pulled her pink canister from her purse. "In the public parking lot. All the street parking was taken."

"I'm over that way too." Liz jingled her keys in her hand. "I'll walk with you."

They chatted about the wedding plans until they reached Liz's car. Liz looked down the street toward the parking lot. "It's awfully dark over there. Why don't I drive you to the lot? I'll feel better knowing you're in your car safe and sound."

"I'll take you up on that. Thanks."

A minute later, as Liz pulled into the parking lot, Maggie caught sight of her own car and her heart froze. "Oh Liz, look at my car!"

The Jetta's driver's-side door was slightly ajar, and cracks radiated from a softball-size hole in the window.

"Don't touch anything," Liz said, putting her car into park and digging her cell phone out of her purse. "I'm calling 911."

Maggie scanned the parking lot for any movement, but it was still. "I have to see what they've done." She pushed the button on her key fob to unlock the Jetta, then exited Liz's car, pepper spray in one hand and cell phone in the other.

As Maggie approached her car, she switched on her phone's flashlight. Heart pounding, she shined the light through the hole in the window. "There's something in the front passenger seat," she shouted to Liz. She pocketed the pepper spray, then pulled a tissue from her coat pocket and put it between her hand and the handle as she opened the door.

Recoiling from the scene in the car, Maggie's hand flew to her mouth and she screamed.

A decapitated antique doll was in the seat, accompanied by a note: *Let the dead rest in peace or you'll be sorry.*

13

Maggie's tissue fell to the pavement and blew across the parking lot as a police car pulled in.

The car screeched to a halt, then Officers Linton and Crosby jumped out and hit the ground running.

"Mrs. Watson, are you all right?" Officer Crosby drew Maggie away from the Jetta as Robert circled around it with a flashlight.

"Physically, yes."

"Who's in the other car?"

"Liz Young. She drove me back to get my car after the meeting because it was so dark."

"She's a good friend." Officer Crosby waved Liz over to them.

"She is," said Maggie, her heart rate beginning to normalize.

"So, tell me exactly what happened," Officer Crosby said as Liz approached.

Maggie described the walk to the meeting and her relief when Liz offered to drive her to the lot. She answered the usual questions, and Officer Crosby jotted down notes while Officer Linton continued his search of the Jetta.

"I got out of Liz's car to look at the damage to my car while she called 911. When I peeked through the hole in the driver's-side window, I saw something in the passenger seat. I'd just opened the door and found—"

She looked up and stopped talking as Officer Linton slowly opened the passenger-side door of the Jetta with a gloved hand and lowered his head inside.

A few seconds later his head reappeared. "Crosby, I think you'd better look at this," he called.

"Stay here," she said, motioning for Maggie and Liz to remain near Liz's car.

Officer Crosby peered into the Jetta. When she backed out of the doorway, her face showed unabashed disgust.

"What in the world is in there?" Liz grabbed Maggie's arm.

Maggie's lip quivered. "An antique doll. Decapitated. And a note telling me to let the dead rest in peace or I'd be sorry."

"Who would do something like that? It's repulsive!"

"We've been hearing from you a lot lately, Maggie," Officer Linton said as he approached Maggie and Liz.

"No offense, but I'd be happy to not see you quite so often." Maggie managed a smile.

"None taken." The officer looked at Liz. "I'm glad you were with Mrs. Watson when she discovered the car burglary. Thank you for calling 911. Maggie doesn't always do that right away." He shot a pointed glance at her.

"Anytime." Liz shivered in the night air.

"We'll bag up evidence now," Officer Linton continued. "We can escort you back to Sedgwick Manor when we're done."

I don't need Dad and Daphne seeing another police car at the manor. "Thank you, but I don't need a police escort. I'm fine. Really. If you'll stay while I make sure the car starts, I'll get home myself. It's not far." Maggie toyed with her keys. "I'll park in the garage tonight and take it to the repair shop first thing tomorrow. I promise."

Officer Linton opened his mouth to speak but closed it without uttering a word. He cleared his throat. "Make sure you call us at the first sign of trouble."

"Don't worry, Officer Linton," Liz said. "I'll follow her home and see she arrives safely. If we run into trouble, I'll call you again." She eyed Maggie. "Don't argue, or I'll make you take the police escort."

Maggie was too tired to protest.

. . . .

The next morning, Maggie looked longingly at the coffee cup on The Busy Bean logo as she led her father and Daphne to the café door. She cringed as the bell above the door jangled and prayed caffeine would take care of the headache jackhammering on her skull. She hadn't slept well, mostly because visions of decapitated dolls danced in her head. The bride and groom had to be at the church to meet with Pastor Young at nine o'clock, so sleeping in wasn't an option. Coffee was the next best thing.

Judging by the sympathetic looks she received when they walked into the coffee shop, word of the car burglary had preceded them.

They were barely inside when Daisy rushed to greet them. "Everybody's wondering about you." She leaned close. "Is it true? Your car was filled with decapitated dolls last night?"

Ah, small-town gossip. "Not quite. One headless doll sat in the passenger side." Maggie didn't mention the threatening note. "The ordeal cost me a sleepless night and $400 insurance claim to replace the window. It's supposed to be fixed tomorrow morning."

Daisy waved them to the window table. "I'll be over as soon as I ring up the Gales' check," she said, nodding toward the elderly couple waiting at the register. "I'll bring coffee."

The trip to the table took longer than usual because several people stopped Maggie to ask about her well-being.

"I think you should stand up on the table and announce the condition of your car and your emotional state," Daphne said, grinning as she sat in the chair Neil had pulled out for her. "Then you can answer all of their questions at one time."

Maggie grinned despite the pounding in her head. "I suppose Daisy is taking care of that as we speak." Maggie nodded toward her gossip-loving friend, who was scurrying from one table to the next.

"She's like a bee humming from flower to flower," Daphne said.

Neil stared at the coffee cups at the next table. "I hope she buzzes this way with the coffeepot pretty soon."

They were still laughing when Daisy materialized with an insulated carafe in one hand and three cups in the other. "Do you need a menu?" She filled their mugs, and Maggie promptly burned her tongue when she snatched her cup and took a hasty sip.

Neil surveyed the plates at a neighboring table. The three sixty-something women were eating pastries. He raised his eyebrows. "What do you recommend?"

"Jack makes a killer egg sandwich," Daisy said. "We serve a lot of those."

"Works for me." He lifted his cup. "And please keep the coffee coming."

Maggie ordered a muffin and fruit and Daphne followed suit.

Daisy leaned in to Maggie. "Did you see the ladies at the table behind you? They're dying to know when you'll have the Twisdem items for sale. What should I tell them?"

Maggie peeked over her shoulder and took in the trio of women wearing pastel sweater sets that, although different colors, looked as though they had come from the same high-end catalog. "Our furniture movers came yesterday, so everything is on the sales floor now."

"I'll let them know," Daisy said, straightening up. "And I'll be right back with your food."

Maggie updated the bride and groom on the wedding plans and answered Daphne's questions without giving away the specific details. Nor did she tell them she'd spoken to her father's siblings and Daphne's daughter on the phone before leaving the manor. All of them planned to attend the wedding despite the last-minute notice. Maggie smiled and kept the secret to herself.

Several tables emptied and the noise level dropped. Maggie lowered her voice accordingly. However, the ladies at the next table did not, making it hard not to overhear their conversation.

"I'd like to get my hands on a couple of things from the Twisdem Mansion," the woman wearing yellow said. "I remember attending a holiday party or two before the infamous crash."

Maggie cocked her head to listen.

"That night changed Marilyn's life forever," her companion in turquoise said. "It was almost fifty years ago, but I still remember feeling just awful saying good-bye when she left for that facility in Switzerland. The whole situation was such a tragedy for her."

"And things aren't any better now." The lady wearing pink straightened up. "I was positively shocked that day I recognized her at Fair Winds when I went to visit Mom. Marilyn's eyes looked glazed over and, although she tried to speak, I heard only gibberish. My ninety-three-year-old mother is in better shape."

Maggie's eyes flew open as she realized what the woman had said. Marilyn Twisdem hadn't died in 1970. And she was currently living just a few streets from where Maggie sat drinking coffee.

The ladies' conversation continued. "Fair Winds is nice enough," the woman wearing turquoise said. "But really, that family still has gobs of money. Marilyn should be at home with private nurses around the clock, not wasting away all alone so her daughter Blair and that smarmy son-in-law can play lady and lord of the manor."

"Well," the lady in pink said, "when I saw her that day, her son-in-law, Forbes, was there. He acted as though he was doing her a favor putting her in that place. I tell you, if I ever come across Blair and Forbes Easton on the street, they'll get a piece of my mind."

Maggie looked at her father and Daphne and mouthed, "Do you hear this?"

For a moment, Daphne's attention moved to the table next to the three women. She motioned to Maggie and murmured, "The man at the table next to them seems as shocked as you. Horrified even."

Maggie slowly shifted in her chair and turned her head far enough to see the table's occupant. When she reached the halfway point, she found herself looking straight into the piercing eyes of Fedora Man.

. . . .

Maggie sat in the back of her father's rented sedan and fumed. If her car had been ready, she could have followed Fedora Man and maybe learned something about him. As it was, though, he had scurried out of the café in a flash. But thanks to the previous night's vandalism, Maggie was stuck without a car. She looked at her watch. Neil and Daphne had plenty of time to drop Maggie by the nursing home and make it to the church on time. "Dad, do you mind dropping me by Fair Winds Nursing Home before you head to your meeting? I'd like to look in on Marilyn Twisdem."

He peered at his daughter in the rearview mirror. "Where is it?" He followed her directions and soon they were on top of a bluff overlooking the ocean.

"Thanks for the ride, Dad," Maggie said as she opened her door.

"No problem. I'll text you when we leave the church."

"Sounds good. I'll be waiting for you." The gleam in her father's eyes made Maggie smile. "Have fun planning your service."

"And I know you're determined to learn more about the Twisdems, but be careful what you ask in there. People don't always take it kindly when strangers start asking questions." His eyes held hers. "I mean it."

"I will. I promise."

"Good." Neil grinned. "I want you in one piece when we go to the Cole Loveren concert tonight."

Relieved the tension was broken, Maggie laughed. "I'm glad you have your priorities straight. Bye, Dad," she said and turned toward the building.

She entered the electronic doors into a posh foyer decorated in rich green and gold. Potted trees were nestled between intimate sitting areas. *This looks pretty ritzy for an institution.*

"May I help you?" A pretty blonde woman smiled at Maggie through the window at the reception desk.

"Good morning. I'm here to see Marilyn Twisdem."

"Twisdem?" The receptionist seemed momentarily confused, but then her face brightened. "Oh, you mean Mrs. Howland."

"Marilyn Twisdem Howland." *So that's her last name.*

"This is my first week. I'm still learning names." She handed Maggie a clipboard with a pen attached by a cord. "Please sign in here, and I'll get someone to take you to Mrs. Howland."

Maggie paced around the lobby a few minutes until a buzzer sounded and a plump woman in casual nurse's garb walked through the door. "Mrs. Watson?"

"I'm Maggie Watson." She stood and approached the nurse.

"I'm Sheila. I'll take you to Mrs. Howland."

"How is she?"

Sheila held the door open for Maggie. "Today is a good day. She's in the solarium. Don't be surprised if she doesn't recognize you. Her memory comes and goes."

"Thanks for the warning."

They stopped in the doorway of the solarium, and Sheila pointed to a frail, gray-haired woman hunched over in a wheelchair next to a bench. "Sadly, she rarely has visitors other than her son-in-law."

"She looks so lonely." Maggie couldn't take her eyes off the woman she'd presumed was dead. "Do you think she'd be up to a reader coming every so often?"

"I think so, but understand she's not always alert. It would be good for her to have more visitors, though."

"Do I need to file a schedule, or can I come anytime?"

"Anytime between ten a.m. and seven p.m. would work fine. Thank you for your interest." Sheila looked down at her watch. "I'll let you visit."

Maggie watched Marilyn from afar to see if she interacted with anyone, but the older woman only stared at a corner of the room filled with lush green plants and a waterfall. She should have brought a small gift or a treat to offer her.

"Hello, Marilyn," Maggie said, sitting on the bench next to the wheelchair. "My name is Maggie. How are you today?"

Pity washed over Maggie as Marilyn gazed at her with dull, nearly colorless eyes.

Marilyn's fine gray hair had been cropped short, too short, probably because it was easier to keep clean. "I don't know you."

Maggie smiled. Marilyn was more aware of her surroundings than she looked. "You're right. But I'm a friend of Ina Linton and Ruth Harper. Do you remember them?"

"Ina? Not here. No Ruth."

"But they were your friends, right?"

Marilyn blinked. "I don't remember."

"I'd like to be your friend too." Maggie looked around the room for a magazine, book, or brochure to read. Nothing. A man with aged hands was reading a newspaper on a bench about fifteen feet away, but his paper was the only reading material Maggie saw. She moved closer to Marilyn. "Next time I'll bring a book and read to you. Would you like that?"

"Read? Okay." Marilyn once again stared across the room, appearing hypnotized by the waterfall. "Where's my brother?"

Maggie froze. *Doesn't Marilyn remember the accident? I can't tell her he's dead.* "Marilyn, I don't know your brother."

Marilyn murmured something unintelligible, and her head bobbed.

"Maggie?" Maggie looked up to find Sue Dixon, a friend from church, staring down at her. "I thought that was you."

"Sue, how are you?" Maggie hugged her. "I haven't seen you in a while."

"I haven't been in church regularly since I started working here. I pull a lot of Sunday shifts."

Maggie was thrilled to know someone on staff. "How long have you been working here?"

"About two months. I like it better than the hospital because I get to know the patients. And it's a beautiful facility."

"It is, especially this area," Maggie said.

"I like to spend my break time in here where I can sit by the waterfall and relax." Sue motioned for Maggie to follow her a few steps away. "I heard what Marilyn said to you. Are you aware Marilyn's parents and brother died in a car crash when she was a college student?"

"I know. I did some research on the family after purchasing pieces from the Twisdem Mansion."

"I figured you did, but I overheard her comments and thought I'd better explain. Sometimes Marilyn reverts to her childhood and talks about her parents and brother like they're still here. For whatever reason, she's blocked the accident out of her memory."

Maggie's cell phone buzzed with an incoming text. "Excuse me a second. This might be my dad saying he's coming to pick me up." She dug her phone from her purse and read the message. "I need to go. He's on his way, but I'll be back. I'm going to start reading to her."

"I'm glad, Maggie." Sue looked at Marilyn. "She doesn't get many visitors."

"Now she has me." Maggie stepped back to Marilyn and kneeled down beside the wheelchair. "I have to go now, Marilyn, but I'll be back soon with one of my favorite books."

Marilyn dipped her head forward. "Read."

"We'll read soon. Good-bye for now."

Sue walked Maggie to the solarium door. "Your visits will be good for her. I look forward to seeing you here."

"It was great catching up." Maggie hugged her friend, then tugged open the door. "See you soon."

Outside the solarium, Maggie's boots struck the polished floors, creating an echo as she walked down the hallway. Marilyn's strange demeanor bothered her. *Is it simply old age, or is something else going on?* Maggie was both afraid and determined to find out.

14

"**M**an, this is a more civilized venue than the first Cole Loveren concert I went to." Neil stopped in his tracks in the middle of Portland's State Theatre lobby.

Maggie laughed, shrugging out of her coat and folding it over her arm. "I guess it would be a little different from a muddy field on a dairy farm in New York State."

"What? Oh, I wasn't at Woodstock, and neither was Cole Loveren. In August 1969, I was about to begin college. And he didn't become popular until 1971 or so." Neil surveyed the opulent lobby. "I was in a wet field near the university when I saw him two years later, though. It was a muddy mess, but we had a blast."

"This is a far cry from any field, muddy or otherwise." Daphne's wide-eyed gaze traveled up one of the large columns to the mural of birds and ladies in the dome of the lobby. "Incredible. Love the Moorish and art deco architecture." She grabbed her fiancé's arm. "We should get a program to keep as a memento of our pre-wedding activities. What do you think?"

"Sure, honey," Neil said.

Daphne's smile fell as she assessed the crowd gathering in the lobby. A long queue extended from the souvenir table. "Maybe we ought to wait until after the concert."

James lightly touched Maggie's arm. "Why don't you and Daphne go find our seats? They're on the floor about a third of the way down. Your dad and I can stand in line to get programs. Everyone have your tickets?"

"Yep," Maggie said. "We'll see you inside."

Maggie and Daphne chatted like old friends as they waited in line to enter the auditorium. When they walked through the door, Daphne clapped her hands like a child. "What a gorgeous theater. I haven't seen one like this for years."

Standing a few paces inside the doorway between the lobby and auditorium, Maggie took in the splendor of the old theater with its ornate scrollwork. She pointed into the auditorium. "I think our seats are just off the aisle on the right side."

She paused to let Daphne walk ahead of her. Before Maggie could take a step to follow, however, pain shot up her right arm as it was jerked and twisted behind her. Hot breath moistened her ear as a low voice growled, "Leave the Twisdem family alone, or you'll be found at the bottom of a ravine too."

"Who are you?" Unable to break free, Maggie pushed against her assailant and leaned her head back as far as she could, trying to see his face. It was no use. His grip was unyielding.

An instant later, she was released and hurled forward, her fall stopped by Daphne's back. The two women nearly fell to the floor as the man disappeared into the crowd.

"Maggie?" Daphne reached out to steady Maggie. "What happened?"

"It's fine." Maggie took a deep breath and picked her coat up off the floor where it had fallen. She wasn't about to scare Daphne. "I stepped on his foot. I guess it hurt."

"That was quite an overreaction, wasn't it?" Daphne stood with her hands on her hips as people pushed by her.

"I won't let it spoil our evening. Let's find our seats." Still shaken, Maggie stepped forward to test her footing. "Nothing injured. No harm done."

The woman behind them reached out and touched Maggie's shoulder. "Are you sure you're okay? My husband took off to try and find the guy who did that."

Maggie managed a weak smile and nodded. "I'm fine. Thank you for asking. I am ready to sit down, though."

Maggie's heart rate was nearly back to normal when they discovered their seats were the first four off the aisle. She gratefully sank down in the farthest seat, leaving the two closest to the aisle for her father and Daphne.

"Are you sure you're all right?" Daphne sat down next to her.

"I'm fine." Maggie scanned the audience. *Surely the guy who grabbed me is long gone by now. But who is he?* "Sit here for now so we can chat, but I'd like you and Dad to take those other seats for the concert. That way you can dance in the aisle if the mood strikes."

Daphne placed her hand on Maggie's arm and squeezed lightly. "Your dad said you had one of the biggest hearts of anyone he's ever met. I can see why. Thank you for everything, especially for accepting me."

"You're good for Dad. You've gotten him to lighten up. And do dishes." Maggie patted Daphne's hand. "I never thought that would happen."

"He was pretty set in his ways when I met him, but he's learned to enjoy himself." Daphne glowed. "He brings me down to earth and I lighten him up. We fit together that way."

Neil shuffled to the seat next to Daphne and held out a program. "Your souvenir, my dear."

Daphne jumped up and hugged him. "Thank you, sweetheart."

The house lights dimmed as James arrived, and they all took their seats.

James leaned into Maggie. "Your dad will enjoy this. Cole Loveren is definitely his favorite musician."

Maggie chuckled. "And you know this how? You just met him two hours ago."

"Because while we were standing in line, he gave me

an enthusiastic mini-lecture about Cole Loveren worthy of a college class."

"Ladies and gentlemen," announced an unidentified voice, "the State Theatre proudly presents music legend Cole Loveren."

A tall man with long gray hair spilling over his shoulders walked into the spotlight with his guitar and sat on the lone stool. He began to sing, his voice pleasant and slightly raspy. He picked up the tempo and Maggie recognized the song from the album they'd played in the library.

"Hello, Portland!" As a four-piece band joined Loveren, the stage exploded in light and the auditorium filled with sound. The audience roared as he stood up and raised the microphone. "Are you ready to rock?"

Maggie was soon lost in her father's favorite music. Neil had always described it to her as rock, country, soul, and blues all rolled into one. Hearing it performed live, Maggie understood what he meant. Letting the recent threats and stress slip from her mind, she was pulled into her father's world. She could recognize each style in the music. As the band played song after song about life, love, change, and redemption, Maggie leaned forward from time to time, stealing glimpses of Neil in flashes of light. His head bobbed in time with the music. When the music slowed to a ballad, he took Daphne's hand and kissed it. Maggie looked away, embarrassed to have intruded on such a private moment.

When Cole Loveren and his band finished the last of three encore songs, Maggie allowed herself to think of the man who had threatened her before the concert. She wouldn't let him ruin this night for her father. She was surrounded by people. She felt safe with Neil, James, and Daphne. Tomorrow was soon enough to tell them.

"That was fantastic, Maggie." Neil swept her into a hug before she stepped into the aisle. "It was the best gift ever."

Joy filled Maggie's heart and temporarily displaced the fear. But as they stepped into the aisle, despite the futility of it, Maggie once again searched the crowd for the man who had grabbed her earlier. She tried to shake off dread as she shrugged into her coat.

By the time they reached the car, it was nearing eleven o'clock. Maggie yawned despite the cold, thankful James was driving. She'd probably be asleep before they were beyond Portland's city limits. A few minutes later, she closed her eyes as Neil and Daphne chatted and laughed softly in the back seat. The soundtrack of their happiness eased Maggie's mind, and peace filled her as she nodded off.

. . . .

Maggie and James drove through a green, lush countryside, humming along to a Cole Loveren song on the radio. Sunshine warmed her face through the window, and she felt peaceful and contented.

Suddenly, the car lurched, and a scream pierced the air.

"Maggie." A hand nudged her shoulder, but the voice didn't belong to James. It was her father. "Maggie, wake up. We have trouble."

Surely I'm dreaming.

"Maggie!" Neil's voice was louder.

Maggie opened her eyes and shook off sleep. James frantically steered the car, attempting to keep it on the road as something scraped the rear left side. She sat up straight and looked at James as the car was bumped from the rear again. Her eyes widened. "What's happening?"

Neil put his hand on her shoulder and squeezed. "Let James handle this. Someone has been following us since we left Portland. After we turned off the highway toward Somerset Harbor, he began tailgating. When we reached the ravine a couple miles back, he started crowding us to the shoulder of the road."

Terror flamed in her. Maggie twisted in her seat to see her father, his face lit by the screen on Daphne's cell phone as she snapped photos through the back window. "They're trying to kill us?"

"If he wanted to kill us, he would have done it at the narrow curve a mile back." Neil's voice was calm, but his face showed fear.

Daphne snapped another photo. "He dropped back a bit. Oh, here he comes. He's—"

Maggie felt the next jolt in her bones. Then they were spinning. Maggie couldn't get her bearings. Squealing tires. Metal scraping metal. Screaming. The car flew into the air and barreled into the ravine. The world went black.

15

Maggie sniffed and coughed and rolled her head from side to side. She forced her eyes open and was assaulted by bright lights overhead. She groaned. "What happened?"

"You hit your head on the window when the car landed." A paramedic shined a flashlight in her eyes with a small pulsing motion. "Look here, please."

Maggie tried to do as she was told, but her head pounded and the light made it worse. She averted her eyes to the side and realized that she was on a gurney in the back of an ambulance. "Where's my dad?"

"He's fine." The paramedic snapped off the light. "The good news is so are you, although you have your share of bruises."

Maggie closed her eyes and tried to remember what happened before the car went off the road. "And James?"

"I'm right here." James's voice came from outside the ambulance's open rear door. "Your father is with Daphne. They're headed to the hospital in another ambulance."

The paramedic held out her hand. "I'll help you sit up and we'll see how you do."

Maggie grasped the proffered hand and sat up on the gurney. "What happened?"

James hopped into the ambulance and came to her side. "The police are working on that."

Maggie's head felt fuzzy. *Dad, James. Dad's with Daphne.* "What's wrong with Daphne?"

"When the car landed in the ravine, it crashed against a tree and crushed the door on that side of the car." James looked her in the eyes. "They aren't sure of the extent of her injuries."

Maggie grabbed his arm. "James, we have to go to the hospital. Dad and Daphne need me."

He covered her hand with his. "We will as soon as you give your statement to the police and my friend Everett arrives to take us."

Maggie shivered. "James?"

"Yes?"

"Will Daphne be okay?"

James nodded with a wan smile. "I have a feeling it would take more than a little tumble to keep her down."

· · · · · · · · · · · · · · · · ·

When Maggie, James, and Everett walked into the hospital waiting room, they found Neil sitting in a chair, bent over with his elbows perched on his knees, his chin resting in his hands. His eyes were closed as if in prayer.

James and Everett went in search of coffee while Maggie and her father waited for news from Daphne's doctor. The minute hand moved slowly on the clock over the intake desk as Maggie pondered what to say. Neil had never been one for needless chatter. They both knew what it was like to wait what seemed like an eternity for a doctor's update. She'd endured it when her mother had suddenly become ill and died a decade before. Maggie had clung to her father's hand when the grim-faced doctor strode into the emergency room and told them to say their good-byes. But when Richard's aortic aneurism ruptured, her father had already moved to Michigan. Maggie had huddled in the emergency room in Bennington with Emily by her side and prayed for a miracle. It had been Richard's time to go. She didn't think the hole in her heart would ever heal fully, but it had become less tender over time. Her father's heart had strengthened too as he adjusted to living life on his own.

Searching for words, Maggie's mind flipped back to the Bennington emergency room and Emily's calming presence, even as a young teenager. Her daughter had simply taken her hand and said, "I love you, Mom." Maybe those were the only words Maggie needed to say.

She leaned closer and put her arm across his back. "I love you, Dad."

He was still for several seconds. When he turned his head toward her, his eyes were filled with tears. "I love you too, Mags." He brushed the tears away as if it would ease his pain. "I loved your mother with all my heart. Didn't think I'd ever get over losing her. I hid myself away because I didn't want to hurt that way ever again. And then I met Daphne."

Tears stung Maggie's eyes. "You really love her."

"I do. We have a different kind of love, perhaps, but it's real. She makes me have fun."

"You deserve to be happy, Dad. Daphne loves you. I can tell by the way she looks at you." The truth of her words hit home.

He shifted in his seat and looked into Maggie's eyes. "You deserve to be happy too. Your heart is too big to keep to yourself." He cleared his throat. "Richard was a good man. He cherished you and Emily. He'd want you to heal and find love with someone else. Let it happen, Maggie."

"Dad, I—"

"Here's your coffee, Maggie." She looked up to find James standing over her with two disposable cups. "Any word?"

Did he hear what Dad said? "Thank you, I really need this." She took the cup from him. "Nothing yet."

"Here's yours, sir." Everett handed a cup to Neil, who accepted it with a grateful nod.

Maggie gasped at a sudden realization. "James! Your Mercedes!"

He shook his head at her. "Of all the silly things to be worried about right now, Maggie. Cars are replaceable. People are not."

A short, slight man in a white doctor's coat walked through the double doors into the ER reception area. "Mr. Segal? I'm Dr. Vidal."

Neil stood. "How is she?"

"She'll be fine. We put a few stitches in the laceration on her head." The doctor rubbed a hand over his left temple area to demonstrate. "She'll have a headache for a day or two. Stitches can come out in about four days."

"When can we take her home?"

"I want to admit her overnight for observation because of the head injury. If all goes well, she should be released before noon tomorrow."

Neil ran a hand through his hair and took a deep breath. "May I stay with her?"

"Ring the bell at the door and they'll take you back. She's transferring to a room." Dr. Vidal stifled a yawn. "The hospitalist will be around to see her in the morning."

As the doctor walked away, James and Everett said good night to Maggie's father and moved closer to the exit. Maggie held back. "Dad, she'll be all right," she said. "You're going to have a beautiful life together."

"I believe you're right." He wrapped her in a hug. "I'll call you when she's being released."

Maggie watched her father disappear through the doors into the examination room area. As she turned toward James and Everett, a man built like a bulldog pushed by Everett and dashed out the exit. *Something about him looks familiar.*

She hurried to the doors. "Did you see the man who walked out the door just now?"

James looked up from the phone in his hand and shook his head. "I'm sorry. I was checking my e-mail."

"I caught a glimpse, but I couldn't pick him out of a lineup." Everett gazed out the glass door a moment, then looked at Maggie. "Why?"

James returned the phone to his pocket. "What is it, Maggie?"

"I don't know. He looked familiar, but I can't place him."

Everett's eyebrows rose. "Did he say anything to you?"

Maggie shook her head and yawned. "It's been a long night and I'm tired. Maybe I'm imagining things."

Everett glanced out the glass doors. "Want me to see if he's outside?"

"That's not necessary," Maggie said. "I'm ready to go home."

James addressed his friend. "Considering what happened tonight, I think it's a good idea for me to stay inside with Maggie while you pull the car up under the portico."

As he spoke, Maggie thought long and hard about what her father had said about moving on.

. . . .

Maggie woke the next morning to an insistent Snickers perched on her stomach, licking her nose.

"Good morning to you too." She yawned as Snickers leaped to the floor and trotted out the door, presumably to the kitchen. Maggie rested her head on the pillow and replayed the prior evening's events in her head. *Maybe if I'd told James about the man who accosted me before the concert, then the accident never would have happened.* She'd blacked out as the car left the road, but she remembered her dad saying the SUV had followed them and bumped the car while she was asleep. *And who was the man I saw leaving the hospital last night?*

The phone beside her bed rang and Maggie rolled on her side to answer it. "Hello?"

"Mrs. Watson?"

"Yes?"

"This is Bob, the mechanic. Your new window is installed. You can pick up your car any time before five o'clock today."

"My car?" All she could think of was James's Mercedes landing in the bottom of the ravine after the concert last night and Daphne ending up in the hospital.

"You dropped it off yesterday to have a new window put in."

Still disoriented from sleep, Maggie sat up and rubbed her eyes, trying to make sense of the montage of images in her head. *Everything started getting strange after the Twisdem auction. The box of random items showing up outside the shop. Curious, but not scary. Eyes appearing at the library window. Disturbing, but not life-threatening. An attempted break-in at the shop. Could have been bad if I hadn't scared him away. And—*

"Mrs. Watson?" The mechanic's voice broke into Maggie's thoughts. "Are you still there?"

And the decapitated doll in the Jetta. Then last night. "I'm here." Maggie cringed as she recalled the broken doll sitting in the passenger's seat on a bed of glass. "I'll pick up the car as soon as I can. Thank you."

Maggie hung up the phone. *It's one thing to break a car window and destroy a doll, but now people are getting hurt. I've got to figure out how to stop this.*

She looked at the clock on her nightstand and was shocked. When was the last time she'd slept until nine o'clock? She picked up the phone and dialed Carriage House Antiques, thankful June normally arrived an hour before opening.

June picked up on the second ring.

"Good morning, June," Maggie said, sounding perkier than she felt. "Do you have much to do before opening?"

"Not too much, why?"

"Would you have time to help me pick up my car? It shouldn't take too long."

"Sure. How's thirty minutes?" June paused a second. "Maggie, what's wrong? You don't sound like yourself. How was the concert?"

"I'll tell you in the car. Right now I need to make another call and make myself presentable."

"Okay. See you in a few."

Maggie hung up the phone and rubbed the sleep out of her eyes. She was tired and sore, but she was determined to check on Daphne and her dad as well as pay another visit to Marilyn. She dialed her father's cell phone.

"Maggie. How are you?" His voice was strained.

"Moving slowly, but fine. How's Daphne?"

Maggie listened to her father's update on Daphne's condition. She'd slept well, eaten a little scrambled eggs and toast, and had a raging headache. The doctor hadn't been in yet.

"Don't worry about us," Neil said. "Go on with your plans. We'll call you when Daphne's discharged."

"Okay." Time was speeding by and Maggie wanted to freshen up before June arrived. "Give my best to Daphne and I'll talk to you later. I love you."

"Will do. Love you too."

Maggie hobbled to the shower and turned the spigots, willing the water to banish her aches and pains. Twenty minutes later, she was fully dressed and standing outside in her coat with a book tucked under her arm.

June's SUV came to a stop in the circular drive and Maggie climbed into the front passenger seat.

"*The Count of Monte Cristo.*" June eyed the book. "Catching up on the classics, are we?"

"Cute." Maggie closed the door. "The book is for Marilyn.

I've decided to start reading to her once or twice a week. She looked pitiful when I saw her."

"Marilyn?"

"As in Marilyn Twisdem Howland."

"No way you're reading to a ghost. Didn't she die from the infamous car crash?"

Maggie explained the conversation she'd overheard at the coffee shop and her subsequent visit to Fair Winds Nursing Home. "Marilyn isn't in great shape, but she's alive."

"Wow, that's a new twist to the story." June put the car in gear. "Now, tell me what happened last night."

Maggie recounted the threat at the concert, the accident, and the subsequent trip to the hospital.

"I'm worried for you, Maggie. I know you love researching antiques and telling their stories to our customers, but someone out there doesn't want you messing with the Twisdems." June pulled up in front of the auto repair shop. "Will you please leave this one alone? We work well together. I don't want to break in another shop owner."

"I can't. I'm worried about Marilyn. Whatever is going on, it must be connected to her." Maggie put her hand on the door handle.

"Strange things were happening before you discovered she was still alive."

"I know, but nobody tried to kill me until then." Maggie opened the door. "Thanks for the ride."

Maggie pushed open the burgundy door to the old general store building now home to Auld's Automotive. Auld's was the cleanest, most organized mechanic shop she'd ever seen. Repairs were done by Bob Auld in a two-bay building behind the office, but business was transacted at the front counter by his wife, Kat.

"May I help you?" Kat's dark auburn hair contrasted with her milky skin.

Maggie strolled to the counter. "I'm Maggie Watson. Bob called this morning and said my car is ready."

"It is. Bob wanted to talk to you. I'll call him in." Kat pulled a yellow paper from a wooden box and placed it on the counter in front of Maggie. "You can take a peek at the invoice."

While Kat summoned her husband, Maggie scanned the invoice, noting the extras Bob had checked: antifreeze, oil, and wiper fluid. To pass the time, she browsed the store aisles filled with gadgets and containers of various automotive fluids.

She pulled a bottle of antifreeze off the shelf and read the label. *Harmful or fatal if swallowed or inhaled. Do not drink antifreeze or solution. If ingested, seek medical attention immediately.*

"Mrs. Watson?"

"Call me Maggie, please." Maggie returned the bottle of antifreeze to the shelf.

"Don't worry about your antifreeze. I checked it. The level is fine. All I did was top off your wiper fluid."

"I was reading the warning label. Pretty scary." Maggie thought of the occasional news articles she'd seen about antifreeze used as a poison. "How could someone accidentally ingest this stuff?"

Bob's blue eyes clouded. "Unfortunately, it's rather easy. Antifreeze is readily available. It's a pretty green color and it has a sweet taste. There have been sad cases of pets getting into antifreeze spilled on a driveway, which is why Diesel over there is not allowed in the garage either here or at home," he said, nodding to the Siberian husky curled on a mat on the other side of the aisle. "Animals are attracted to its color and taste, as are people."

Maggie shivered. "Must be an awful way to die."

"It is, whether it happens slowly or quickly," he said. "Some of the danger is because symptoms mirror so many diseases. Dizziness, fatigue, blurred vision, slurred speech, lack of alertness, and nausea are just a few. It's best to keep antifreeze locked away. And let me know if you suspect a leak."

Maggie shivered when she thought of Marilyn's slurred words and lethargy at Fair Winds the previous day. Could she be suffering from antifreeze poisoning? *Come on, Maggie. That's a bit of a stretch, even for you.* "I think I'll let you keep the antifreeze here and I'll bring my car in when I need it," Maggie said.

"Good plan." Bob smiled. "By the way, your car is in great shape. I wish all my customers kept their vehicles in such pristine condition."

"Thank you." Maggie held up the invoice. "I suppose I should pay my bill so you two can get back to it."

. . . .

"Good morning, Mrs. Watson." The Fair Winds receptionist greeted Maggie before she reached the window. "Are you here to visit Mrs. Howland?"

"I'm here to read to her." She held up the book. "Maybe *The Count of Monte Cristo* will bring a twinkle to her eye."

"Count what?" The girl's face was blank.

"It's one of my favorite books. I thought Mrs. Howland might enjoy hearing it." Maggie bent her head to sign the visitor registry. *Don't people read the classics anymore?* When she looked up, the receptionist was staring at her with a pained expression. Maggie touched her hand to her right cheek, bruised where it had slammed against the car window when the car careened off the road. "It looks worse than it is. I was in a car wreck last night. The car is pretty mangled, but the rest of us are fine, thank God."

The receptionist grimaced. "Ouch. I'm glad everyone is okay." She retrieved the clipboard. "Sheila will be out to get you in a moment."

"Thank you." Maggie drifted over to a painting hanging above the love seat. The seascape had been painted by a local artist whose work she'd had in the shop from time to time. As she studied its composition, Maggie realized the scene was the cliff behind Fair Winds Nursing Home.

"Beautiful, isn't it?" Sheila appeared at her side. "One thing I love about this place, besides the high level of care, is that management goes out of its way to create a soothing environment for our residents."

"It's gorgeous." Maggie turned to the nurse. "How's Mrs. Howland today?"

"Mrs. Howland is having a rough time this morning," she said, escorting Maggie to the inner door. "I hope listening to you read will perk her up some."

"Me too." The buzzer sounded and Maggie's fingers tightened around the book as they walked through the door.

When Maggie paused to turn down the hallway to the solarium, Sheila pointed straight ahead. "She's in her room. It's this way."

"Oh, I was hoping to read in the solarium. It's so peaceful in there."

"I don't think she's up for it this morning."

Maggie cut her eyes toward Sheila.

The nurse held up her hand. "That's all I can say. Privacy laws, you know."

"I understand," Maggie said, uneasiness creeping under her skin.

Sheila stopped in front of room 121. "She probably won't remember you, but don't be alarmed. Your visit will be good for her."

Maggie nodded and followed Sheila into the room.

"Mrs. Howland, you have a visitor." Sheila went to Marilyn's bedside and patted her patient's shoulder. "Maggie Watson came back to read to you."

Maggie went to the bedside and struggled to maintain composure. Marilyn was pale and her eyes were glassy. Maggie managed a smile. "Good morning, Marilyn. I brought one of my favorite books to read, *The Count of Monte Cristo* by Alexandre Dumas."

Marilyn's eyes fluttered open. As she turned her head toward Maggie, the corners of her mouth turned up ever so slightly.

Sheila stepped away from the bed. "I think she remembers you. Thank you for visiting her."

"I'm happy to brighten her day a bit." Maggie pulled a chair up beside the bed as the nurse left the room. She opened the leather-bound book. "'On February 24, 1815 . . .'"

She read the first chapter and paused at the end to check Marilyn's response. Her head was turned toward Maggie, but her eyes had no spark. The earlier smile had faded.

"I enjoyed that so much I'm going to read the next chapter." Maggie continued reading, pausing to hold up a picture of a somber Edmond Dantès for Marilyn to see. "Here's Edmond. A nice illustration, don't you think?"

The older woman's eyes fluttered shut.

Maggie closed the book. "I think that's enough for today," she said, attempting to sound cheerful. "I'll come back soon and read the next chapter." She leaned closer. "I hope you'll be my friend, Marilyn. I want to help you."

Maggie stepped into the hallway and leaned against the wall to collect her thoughts. Once again, Marilyn's poor health troubled her greatly. Was she too sedated? On the wrong medication? Showing early signs of a neurological disease?

Interrupting her musing, Maggie's phone chimed to signal the arrival of a text message from her father: *Daphne cleared to leave hospital. Just need to finish paperwork.*

Pleased with the good news, she replied to her dad immediately: *Great to hear. Let me know when you're ready.*

Maggie walked down the corridor attempting to focus on the positive. She was thrilled Daphne was being released and would be able to continue with wedding plans. She entered the lobby and waved to the receptionist on her way to the front door. She paused briefly in the warmth of the building to pull her keys from her purse. Her hands also closed around the pink pepper spray canister. After her troubling last few days, she felt compelled to carry it as well.

Cold air blasted her in the face as the double doors opened, and she stepped onto the walkway with her to-do list on her mind. With only a few days until the wedding, she had so much to get done.

She was nearly to the Jetta when two hands wrapped around her arm and spun her around. "I want to talk to you," a male voice growled.

He was wearing sunglasses, but she knew exactly who he was. Fedora Man.

"Let me go!" she yelled, bringing a boot down on his foot. He released his grip. She pushed him away and knocked him off-balance, giving her time to activate the pepper spray. She held out her arm and sprayed in his direction. The man's hands flew up and he screamed in pain as the spray penetrated his nose and mouth.

Maggie ran to her car, jumped in, and locked the doors. *Should I go back inside and report him?* She looked at the man crouched down on the pavement, his hands wiping at his face.

She heard squealing tires, and suddenly a black SUV screeched to a halt in front of her. The passenger door was opened from the inside, and Fedora Man scrambled to his feet, got in, and slammed the door shut. With more squealing, the SUV hurtled out of the parking lot. Not too fast for Maggie to notice its scratched and dented front bumper, however.

She frowned, watching the vehicle disappear. *Scratched and dented as though it ran James's Mercedes off the road last night?*

$\mathbf{M}$aggie's phone chimed as she sat in the parking lot, contemplating. She had another text from her father at the hospital: *Should be ready in 20 minutes. Will wait in front of Door B for you.* There was no telling how long she'd be held up if she went back inside the nursing home to file a report about Fedora Man's assault. He was long gone anyway, along with whatever accomplice he had driving that SUV. Maggie determined that it was probably best to go get Daphne for now. There was nothing the Fair Winds staff could do for her.

Maggie drove through Somerset Harbor as her mind raced, frantically debating whether to call the police. Fueled by the stress of the attack, tears welled in her eyes.

Before the teardrops could fall, she pulled over in an alley off Harbor Street and checked her face in the rearview mirror. She gave herself a pep talk. "Don't you dare lose it, Maggie. You can handle this. Dad and Daphne need you." She wiped her eyes with her coat sleeve and breathed in new resolve.

She put her car in gear and inched to the street, but her cell phone rang before she left the alley. Maggie put her car in park and dug the phone out of her purse. "Hello?"

"Maggie, it's James. How's Daphne this morning?"

"She was given her release papers a little while ago. Dad said she's feeling sore, but better. I'm heading to the hospital to pick them up."

"Oh, you have your car back," he said, disappointment evident in his voice. "My car place loaned me a Cadillac to use while the Mercedes is being fixed. It has plenty of legroom.

Why don't I swing by Sedgwick Manor and pick you up?"

Maggie sighed with relief. She didn't want to be alone after the confrontation with Fedora Man, and she always felt safe with James. It was worth the extra step to drop her car off at home and hop into his. "I'd like that. I'm glad your car is fixable."

"Me too, though I'm really enjoying the Cadillac. I'll be there in a few minutes."

Maggie pulled onto Harbor Street and turned right toward Shoreline Drive. With any luck, she'd have just enough time to fix her makeup and hide the evidence of her tears.

. . . .

"Perfect timing." James pulled the Cadillac under the portico in front of the hospital as Neil appeared through the automatic doors with a hospital employee pushing Daphne in a wheelchair.

Daphne was wearing gray sweats under her winter coat. She clutched a bulky white plastic bag across her thighs.

"I didn't even think to bring Daphne a change of clothes." Maggie groaned. "I'm a sorry excuse for a future stepdaughter."

James put the car in park. "Maggie, you're giving Daphne pretty close to the wedding of her dreams with a week's notice. I think that qualifies you for the stepdaughter hall of fame." He took her hand and squeezed. "Don't be so hard on yourself. Your life has been strange since the day of the Twisdem auction."

"Thank you," she said, looking into his eyes. "You've been such a good friend."

"Maggie—"

A sharp rapping on Maggie's window interrupted his words. Neil was peering in at her.

She rolled down the window. "Ready?"

"Very." Her father's eyes were bloodshot. "She's all checked out with marching orders."

The attendant wheeled Daphne down the ramp, and Neil opened the car door. Daphne eased out of the chair and into the car with a groan.

"Have a good day," the attendant said, turning toward the building with the wheelchair.

Maggie watched Daphne settle into the back seat. "Nice threads," she said.

A woozy Daphne smiled. "I didn't want to bother you for clothes, so my nurse suggested Neil check in the thrift store a block away. This is what he brought back to me. Men's extra-large. Sweats are so flattering, aren't they?"

Neil kissed Daphne's cheek. "Sweats or not, you're always a beauty to me." He put his arm around her. "I'm thankful you don't have a concussion."

James turned on an oldies radio channel and they rode the rest of the way home humming to the music. Maggie was glad to avoid talking about the accident. The noon news broadcast came on as the Cadillac pulled up to Sedgwick Manor.

"It's noon already?" Maggie looked at the car's clock.

Maggie and James walked to the front steps as Neil helped Daphne out of the car and escorted her slowly up the walkway. "Daphne, do you feel like eating?"

"No thank you, Maggie," she replied. "Right now I want sleep above all else."

"I understand completely. Please let me know if I can get you something." Maggie went up the steps and unlocked the front door.

From the foyer, Maggie and James watched Neil and Daphne slowly climb the stairs. When they disappeared, James wrapped Maggie in a quick hug. "How are you holding up?" He backed away. "You haven't stopped to rest in days. The Twisdem auction and wedding planning is enough, but add to that an attempted burglary and a car accident, and I'm afraid you're going to collapse."

Marilyn's condition and the incident in the nursing home parking lot flashed through Maggie's mind, but she wasn't ready to talk about it yet. "I'm okay. It's been hectic, but I'm glad I've had time with Dad."

James glanced up the stairs. "Daphne will probably sleep for a while, and I imagine Neil won't want to leave her. Let me take you out to dinner. I promise to have you home early."

Growing more convinced that Marilyn was being drugged or poisoned, Maggie had planned to return to Twisdem Mansion to visit Marilyn's daughter, Blair. She had to admit, however, that a nice relaxing dinner out with James would be a welcome change to the drama of the last couple of days. "I'd like that."

He grinned. "I'll make reservations at The Lobster Quadrille and pick you up at six."

Maggie walked him to the door. "I guess I'd better attack my to-do list in the meantime."

"I was hoping you'd rest, but I should have known better," James said, laughing. He opened the door and trotted down the steps before she had time to react.

Maggie stood at the door and watched until the Cadillac pulled away. As she was closing the door, Snickers ran between her legs and disappeared in the bushes lining the front of the house. "Don't stay out here too long, Snickers," she called. "The temperature is supposed to drop later this afternoon."

She closed the door and walked through the library to the office, then removed her coat and draped it across the back of a chair. She sat down, leaned her head back, and contemplated her conversation with Bob Auld. She had to tell someone her suspicions. But who? If something strange or life-threatening were happening to Maggie, Emily would want to be the first to know. *I need to talk to Blair Easton.*

• • • • • • • • • • • • • • • •

Maggie's nerves were on edge as she approached the Twisdem Mansion, but she appreciated her luck in finding the gates open.

The manor stood as a stately sentinel over the well-kept grounds. Although the family had been reclusive in recent decades, its business interests must have been furthered by someone if the house was still in their name and in such pristine condition.

Maggie parked the car parallel to the two levels of concrete steps leading to the front door. *This is where the craziness started.* With a prayer and her suppositions about Marilyn, Maggie climbed the stairs.

She rang the bell and stepped back as a booming chime echoed inside the house. The door opened several seconds later and a woman in a navy blue business suit opened the door. "May I help you?"

"Hello, my name is Maggie Watson. I own Carriage House Antiques. Are you Blair Easton?"

The woman gave her a condescending smile. "I'm Mrs. Easton's personal assistant. If you're here to buy antiques, I'm afraid the family has sold everything they'd planned to discard."

Discard? What an odd word choice. "I purchased some lovely pieces during the auction and they're now for sale in my shop. But today I'm here to talk with Mrs. Easton about her mother. I won't keep her long, I promise."

"Her mother? What do you need to discuss about her mother?"

Maggie's suspicions surged. "I had a nice visit with her. I wanted to tell Mrs. Easton about it."

"I'm afraid she's resting right now. Do you have a card?"

Maggie rooted around in her purse, pulled out a card, and passed it to the woman. "Please have her call me."

"Glenda, who is it?" An attractive woman in her forties appeared in the doorway and nudged the assistant aside. "Did you say something about my mother?"

"Mrs. Easton, I'm Maggie Watson. I visited your mother yesterday and this morning, and I'd like to tell you about it."

Blair studied Maggie a moment and opened the door wider. "Please come in. We'll talk in the parlor." She turned to her assistant. "That will be all for now. We'll continue our business later."

Blair led the way down the long hallway where antique landscape paintings had hung during the auction. The beautiful pieces had been swapped for a collection of abstract works by an artist Maggie didn't recognize. Most of the gorgeous antiques she remembered from before had been replaced with contemporary furniture.

The parlor, though, was as Maggie imagined it must have been over a hundred years ago, much like the salon and dining room had been when she and June had done their mini tour during the auction. The centerpiece was a harpsichord to the left of the fireplace. The fireside sitting area featured two rococo chairs upholstered in rich red velvet with a cherrywood pedestal table between them.

"Please, sit down." Blair motioned to one chair as she sat in the other. "Tell me about your visit with my mother."

She listened quietly as Maggie talked about attending the auction at the Twisdem Mansion and explained her habit of researching the history of antiques she sold at the shop. "I became enthralled with the family history and searched the newspaper archive for articles about the 1970 wreck that killed your grandparents and uncle. The last article I found was printed a few days after the accident. It said your mother was on life support and not expected to live." Maggie cleared her throat, stalling for time before she continued. "Mrs. Easton, I thought your mother died all those years ago in the car crash. I think a lot of people are under that impression."

Blair didn't move, and Maggie could read nothing in her face. She appeared as regal as royalty, her light brown hair pulled back in a chignon. "Please, call me Blair, and continue your story."

"My father, his fiancée, and I stopped in The Busy Bean for coffee yesterday morning, and we overheard three women talking about your mother. It sounded like they knew her when she was young. One of them mentioned seeing her at Fair Winds Nursing Home and described her as looking . . . unwell." Maggie paused, trying to read Blair's face. "Once I was over the shock of discovering your mother was alive, the meaning of their words sunk in. They were concerned about her."

Blair's green eyes clouded. "Do you think they have a reason to be worried?"

Maggie recounted her experiences at the nursing home and described Marilyn's behavior. "I have no medical training, of course, but she did seem disoriented the first time and incoherent the second." She sat forward on the edge of her seat. "Mrs. Easton, do you know why anyone would want to drug or poison your mother?"

Blair shook her head. "She'd never do anything to make someone want to harm her. My mother is a gentle woman who never quite recovered emotionally after the accident. She met my father while recuperating in Switzerland, and he ran the business from Boston when they returned to the States. She loved him very much and relied on him a great deal. He died a few years ago."

"I'm so sorry," Maggie said.

"Thank you." Blair looked at her hands, then back up at Maggie. "After my father passed, she kept even more to herself than usual, just listening to her records and reading all day. Then, her health began to deteriorate, so my husband suggested she move into Fair Winds for better care. She'd become confused and agitated. We were afraid she'd wander into a remote part of the house, fall, and get hurt. She was having dizzy spells and memory lapses more frequently."

"I see."

"I'm afraid I've not been good about visiting her because it's difficult for me to see her in that place. But I'll go tomorrow."

"I'm glad." Maggie stood and studied Blair's face for any sign she might be lying, but her expression gave up nothing. "Thank you for listening. I thought you should know about my experience."

Blair held out her hand. "Thank you for coming."

Before Maggie moved, the parlor door opened and a handsome man in a well-tailored business suit strolled in the room. He bent down to kiss his wife. "Blair, sweetheart, you didn't mention you were having company today."

Maggie stepped forward and offered a handshake. "I'm afraid I showed up unannounced. I'm Maggie Watson of Carriage House Antiques. I was asking about the history of some of the pieces I purchased."

"I see." He pulled a card out of his coat pocket. "I'm Forbes Easton. Please contact me if you have questions in the future."

"I'll do that," Maggie replied, glancing at the card. The Twisdem Corporation logo was emblazoned in red across the top. "Thank you. I'll be going now."

. . . .

"This is absolutely heavenly," Maggie said, picking a huge chunk of meat from a lobster claw and dredging it through a small cup of melted butter. "This is exactly what I needed after a crazy week. Thank you."

James smiled, his handsome face softened by the candle glowing between them. "I thought you could use a break from the drama."

Maggie loved The Lobster Quadrille with its casual but creative nautical decor and exceptional seafood. She'd been exhausted when she left the Twisdem Mansion and almost cancelled the dinner. But a hot shower, clean clothes, and encouragement from her father and Daphne motivated her to keep the date. Now she was glad she had. James had a calming influence on her.

"Uh-oh, don't look now," James said. "But Forbes Easton just sat down two tables away."

"I didn't realize you knew him."

"I don't. Not really. I met him six months ago at a country club in Portland when I was having lunch with mutual business associates. It's the only time I've ever seen him. And I had no idea he was Marilyn's son-in-law until you told me."

"So much for our peaceful evening." Maggie closed her eyes and took a deep breath. "I'm not going to think about the Twisdem family tonight."

"Good idea," James said. "I've been wanting to tell you about the Sykes place, my latest restoration project. It's this incredible nineteenth-century mansion in New Hampshire. It's practically a castle."

They chatted easily about James's work, the upcoming wedding at Sedgwick Manor, and the town council's approval to annex several acres on the south side. To Maggie's relief, they avoided talking about both the accident and the Twisdem family. She felt relaxed for the first time since attending the auction.

They were perusing the dessert menu when Forbes Easton appeared, his presence looming over their table like a storm cloud. "You needn't read to my mother-in-law anymore. She doesn't need you."

He turned on his heel and returned to his table before Maggie or James said a word.

"I think I'll forego dessert," Maggie said, leaning across the table. "But no way am I going to stop visiting Marilyn Twisdem. Especially not if he wants me to."

. . . .

Maggie took James's arm as he walked her to the front door. The night was cold and clear, and the sky twinkled with stars. With the exception of Forbes's untimely intrusion, the evening had been perfect.

"Thank you for tonight," Maggie said, giving James a quick hug before stepping toward the door. "I had a lovely time."

"I did too." James looked at her carefully. "Maggie, don't push Forbes too hard."

"*Moi?*" Maggie grinned. "Never."

"You're incorrigible, you know that?"

She laughed. "It's one of my most endearing qualities."

James shook his head. "Sometimes," he said, descending the steps. "Please be careful."

Maggie let herself in the door. "Snickers? Where are you, boy?"

Country rock music spilled from the library. "Hi, you two," she said, entering the library to see Neil and Daphne cuddled on the love seat. "How are you feeling, Daphne?"

"Moving slowly, but I'm moving." She had ditched the unflattering sweats in favor of coordinating jewel-toned tunic and leggings.

"You look much better." Maggie looked around the room. "Where's Snickers? He didn't come when I called him." Maggie's heart sank when she saw their puzzled expressions. "He darted out when I was seeing James to the door this afternoon. He never came back?"

"We haven't seen him." Neil pulled Daphne closer. "We were upstairs most of the afternoon and wouldn't have heard or seen him."

Fear gripped Maggie. It was getting colder outside. "I'm going to check out back."

She ran through the house to the kitchen, grabbed a flashlight from the pantry, and dashed out. "Snickers! Here kitty, kitty," she called, moving the light from side to side. "Come on home, Snickers." She stopped and listened for a meow, a hiss, or the rustling of bushes. But the windless night was silent except for waves breaking on the beach.

17

Maggie splashed through the freezing ocean water. "Snickers! Snickers! Where are you?" Her teeth chattered, the cold air and water matching the chill in her heart. "Oh, Snickers. I'm sorry. Come back. I love you." Her words were blown away by the wind.

Maggie woke with a start and doubled over with pain as sweat poured from her face. She shivered and pulled the covers up to her chin, but the shaking continued. The grandfather clock chimed twice from the hallway. What was wrong with her? She was falling, drowning, fading . . .

Pain yanked her from restless sleep. Her stomach was on fire and her head pounded. The chills continued.

Maggie stumbled to the bathroom and splashed water on her face. She filled a glass at the faucet and took a few sips. She leaned against the sink for a few moments to catch her breath, then staggered back to bed and burrowed under the covers.

Daylight was peeking in the window when Maggie woke again.

She remembered what happened the previous night. Forbes had for all intents and purposes told her to leave his mother-in-law alone. She'd come home to find Snickers missing. Her mind flipped to her conversation with Bob Auld about antifreeze. Nausea, vomiting, weakness, and dizziness were all symptoms of several types of poisoning. She'd been warned at the concert. That man had said to leave the Twisdems alone or she'd be found at the bottom of a ravine, and then the accident happened. She went to see Marilyn and Blair, and now this. *Have I been poisoned?*

Maggie's eyes burned with tears. She bowed her head and

murmured a prayer for her cat. Her prayer was punctuated by a rap on the door. "Maggie, are you all right?"

Maggie stumbled to the door and opened it. "I've had better nights."

"Oh my goodness. You're so pale." Daphne put her arm around Maggie and led her back to bed. "What happened?"

Maggie shrugged. "It must have been something I ate combined with worry about Snickers. Have you seen him this morning?"

"I haven't, and your father's been out searching for an hour."

Maggie managed a smile. "You have Dad searching for a cat. You've truly bewitched him."

"Oh, Maggie, your father loves you. We both felt terrible about not looking for him last night."

"You had no way to know he wasn't somewhere in this big house." Maggie rubbed her temples. "How are you feeling?"

"Much better. Not quite up to snuff, but I'm getting there." Daphne pressed on the bandage on her temple. "A bath might help you feel better. Would you like me to draw you one?"

"A bath sounds good."

Maggie crawled under the covers and closed her eyes. A few minutes later, she felt a hand on her shoulder.

"Maggie? Your bath is ready." Daphne walked to the bedroom door. "I'll be back in half an hour to check on you."

By the time Daphne returned, Maggie was reading on the sofa in the sitting room, dressed in a pair of old yoga pants and an oversize T-shirt.

"Oh, you look much better." Daphne sat down in the overstuffed chair and put her feet on the ottoman. "Your dad is back. He didn't find Snickers. I'm so sorry."

"I know he will come back as long as he's not hurt somewhere." Maggie's voice wavered. "I have to believe he's okay."

"Neil will keep looking."

Daphne reached out and pulled a piece of sea glass from the bowl on the table in front of her. "I love the bowls of sea glass and shells sprinkled around this house. There's treasure in every room." She turned the glass over and over in her hand before returning it to the bowl. "If we're both up to it, I do want to discuss some wedding plans today."

Maggie put her book on the coffee table. "I'd like that. I have a checklist we can go over so you can get an idea of the progress we've made."

"We can send Neil out to run errands, if needed. He likes keeping busy." Daphne stood up. "I'm going to go check on him. Come out when you feel up for wedding talk. Do you want to try something to eat?"

"Oh no," Maggie said, shuddering. "I'll be ready for wedding plans much sooner than food."

· · · · · · · · · · · · · · · · ·

An hour later, Maggie joined Neil and Daphne in the living room, where they were sitting on the sofa. He was reading the *Portland Gazette* and she was flipping through an antiques magazine.

"She's alive," Neil announced as Maggie shuffled into the room.

"I feel like I've been hit by a truck, but I'm alive." Maggie carried a legal pad and a file folder.

"Well, that happened to you this week too, though technically that one was an SUV." He jumped up from the sofa. "What can I get you? Tea? Water? Crackers?"

Maggie's stomach twisted at the mention of food. "I think my stomach needs to stay empty for a while, but Daphne and I might need you to run some wedding errands later. Would you be up for that?"

"Anything you need, Mags." He hugged her. "Just ask. I'll have another go at finding Snickers too."

Maggie slowly sank into one of the matching wingback chairs on either side of the sofa. "Thanks, Dad. I'm really worried about him. He usually doesn't stay out overnight. I wish I could stay on my feet longer without getting woozy. I should be out looking for him."

"Are you sure you're up to discussing wedding plans?" Daphne closed the magazine. "We can do this later."

She really is a wonder, this woman my father is marrying. Daphne has five stitches in her head but is more worried about me. "Daphne, there is no 'later.' The wedding is in three days."

Daphne giggled. "My, how time flies."

Maggie shuffled through her folder and remembered the photos she'd taken at the last meeting. "I'll be right back. I need to get my phone. I left it on my dresser."

"I'll get it." Neil said, leaving the room before Maggie could rise from her chair.

Maggie scanned her notes. "Your wedding is truly a group effort. Even the ladies you met at the beauty salon were involved."

"The beauty shop ladies? Really?" Daphne smiled. "Small towns are the best."

"Indeed they are," Neil said, entering the room and dropping the phone in Maggie's outstretched hand.

Maggie opened her photo app and scrolled to the wedding images. "Daisy, my friend who owns the coffee shop, and Maura, the town's librarian, came up with the ideal theme. The rest of us built upon it. You'll love it."

She lifted the phone to show Daphne the flowers for the banister, bouquet, and reception tables, but didn't turn the screen toward her. "How many details do you want? Do you want to know the theme?"

Daphne bit her lip in contemplation. "Yes. No." She groaned in mock frustration. "I don't know."

Maggie laughed. "How about I tell you the theme and show you photos of the food? The flowers and table decorations can be a surprise."

"Perfect," Daphne said, her eyes twinkling.

"Our inspiration is—drumroll please—Sylvia Sterling's wedding!" Maggie paused for effect as Daphne's face lit up. "Your flowers will be a modern twist on her bouquet and arrangements. Liz Young has arranged for the church pianist to provide music—traditional for the service and show tunes for the reception."

"And the food?" Maggie's dad asked.

Maggie scrolled through the photos and opened the first picture of the food table Daisy had set up at the meeting. "Daisy is providing brunch at cost." She gave the phone to Daphne. "Of course, the serving table will be decorated to match the theme."

Maggie noticed that Neil was fidgeting and looked bored. She was impressed he'd lasted this long. "Dad, how about running a few errands for me?" When he nodded, she tore her to-do list in two, detaching the top four items from the rest.

He stood up immediately, his relief obvious. He looked at the list. "Easy enough. I'll look around for the cat before I go." He slid the list into his shirt pocket, then leaned over to kiss Daphne. "You two have fun."

"We will," they replied in unison, watching him walk out of the living room.

"Thank goodness he's gone," Daphne said. "His fidgeting was driving me nuts." The women looked at each other and laughed.

"Dad never was one for decorating or entertaining. He even coined his own word for it—frillary."

"Frillary?" Daphne contorted her face into a funny expression. "As in, excessive frills? There's no such thing when it comes to a wedding. On with the frillary!"

They were discussing the ceremony and reception setup when there was a knock on the door. Maggie opened it to see Ruth, Liz, and Ina loaded down with bags full of wedding supplies.

"We ran into your father at The Busy Bean. Obviously he shares your addiction to coffee," Ina joked. "He said he was getting out of Dodge while his favorite women discussed . . . what was the word? Flippary?"

Ruth laughed. "Frillary. I've never heard the word before, but I'm assuming he'd had enough wedding talk. Men can't handle that stuff very long. They either couldn't care less, or they care even more than the bride does."

"We see it at the church all the time," Liz said, her arms wrapped around a large bag. "People talk about bridezillas, but sometimes the grooms are harder to please than the brides. By the way, this bag has bread and chicken soup in it. Daisy fixed you a care package after your father told her you were feeling poorly. She said it will cure what ails you. I'll take it to the kitchen."

The morning flew by. The bride charmed the members of the Somerset Harbor Historical Society as they refined the details of the wedding ceremony and reception. "Of course, Neil and I want all of you to be there. With the short notice and craziness, we never would've been able to plan this beautiful day without you."

James called around noon. "Maggie, are you all right? Neil said you woke up sick in the middle of the night."

"When did you talk to Dad?" Maggie slowly rose from the chair to seek a quiet spot in her bedroom sitting area.

"Daisy told me when I stopped in for a midmorning coffee."

"Is there anyone in town who doesn't know I'm ill?"

"Maggie, this is serious. Neil also said Snickers disappeared yesterday. It's not out of the question to think someone is trying to hurt you." He paused. "Maggie, I'm worried you've been poisoned. Maybe Snickers too."

Maggie's blood turned cold. She hadn't thought about Snickers being harmed because of her. "We must find Snickers."

"Let someone else find him. I'm going to take you to the emergency room. I'll be there in five minutes."

"Don't worry, James. I don't feel like running a marathon, but I feel better than I did a few hours ago. Besides, I have a room full of friends in full wedding planning mode."

"They'll understand."

"I'm feeling better. Besides, Daisy sent her chicken soup. It has miraculous healing powers."

"You are without a doubt the most hardheaded woman I've ever known."

Maggie managed a chuckle. "It's part of my charm."

"I'm not touching that comment with a ten-foot pole." James sighed. "So you're not on your deathbed. I'll let you get back to the wedding plans, but I'll check on you later."

Maggie ended the call feeling even better than before.

Her friends and soon-to-be stepmother were laughing and chattering when she returned to the planning session.

Liz looked up as Maggie joined the group. "Are you doing all right?"

"I'm fine. It's nothing that some of Daisy's soup and a nap won't cure." Maggie addressed all of them. "Thank you, all of you, for pulling together and making this wedding happen." She waved her hand over the wedding paraphernalia strewn across the coffee table. "We couldn't have done it without you."

Ruth stood up and began refilling her bag. "These two have had a tiring week. We ought to let them rest."

Maggie was ready for peace and quiet. She needed to focus and try to make sense of everything that had happened since the Twisdem auction. When everyone had packed up their supplies, Maggie walked them to the door. "Thank you all again," she said, opening the door to find a florist deliveryman setting a bouquet of flowers on her doorstep.

"Are you Maggie Watson?"

"I am," Maggie said. "Who would send me flowers?"

"I don't know, I just deliver them," the man snapped, turning on his heel. Maggie watched the man scurry down the path. He didn't stop or turn around to answer. There was no delivery van in sight.

Maggie stepped back inside and closed the door, knowing her friends would want to see the flowers. She pulled back the green tissue paper and found a dozen white gladioli, a flower Maggie had always associated with funerals. She shuddered and plucked out the card lodged between two stems.

Liz placed a hand on Maggie's arm. "What does it say?"

Maggie swallowed. "It says, 'Let sleeping dogs lie or you'll be sorry.'"

18

The friends were silent for several seconds and then began talking all at once. Ruth let out the loudest whistle Maggie had ever heard. "Ladies, let Maggie have a chance to breathe."

Maggie mouthed "thank you" to Ruth before addressing the group. "I don't know who sent these flowers, but I trust the Somerset Harbor Police Department to find out. The best thing for you to do is go on with your afternoon. I'll let you know what happens."

Liz's eyes were glued to the flowers. "We're worried about you."

"I'll be fine. Daphne is here with me and my father will be back very soon." She held the flowers with the blooms toward the floor. "I'll keep in touch, I promise."

Liz moved through the group to stand by Maggie. "I'd like to lead us in a brief prayer for Maggie, her father, and Daphne before we leave." She looked at Maggie. "What do you think?"

Maggie nodded. "Please do."

The women huddled together, and Liz said a short prayer for Maggie's safety, as well as that of her father and Daphne.

Maggie hugged each woman as she walked out the door. When she closed the door behind them, she sat on the bottom step of the stairway and dialed the police.

. . . .

"I think we have everything we need." Officer Linton shoved his notepad into his back pocket. "I'm glad you called us so quickly. For once."

Officer Crosby handed Maggie one of her cards. "You've

been through the ringer lately. If you think of anything else or have any questions, please give me a call."

"I do have one more thing." She sighed as tears welled in her eyes. "My cat, Snickers, is missing. Will you please keep an eye out for him? He doesn't usually stay gone this long."

Officer Linton pulled his notepad back out, flipped it open, and removed the small attached pen. "Do you have a photo of him?"

"Yes, in the office. I'll be right back." Maggie dashed through the library and grabbed the framed photo of Emily and Snickers she kept on the desk. When she returned, she handed it to Officer Linton and said, "I took this during Emily's Christmas break."

He stared at the picture a minute. "May we take the photo?"

"Sure. Let me get it out of the frame."

He handed it back and Officer Crosby moved toward the door. "I'm going to look around outside."

"Okay." Officer Linton watched Maggie remove the back of the picture frame. "When did you last see the cat?"

"Yesterday afternoon. He ran out the door when James Bennett opened it to leave." Her voice broke. "None of us have seen him since. With the cold weather and craziness going on around here, I'm really worried."

"Is he normally an indoor cat?"

Maggie sniffled. "He's both. Snickers likes to have free run of the house and the neighborhood, but he's never been gone this long before."

Maggie heard a light tap on the door and Officer Crosby entered the foyer.

Hope welled inside her. "Any sign of Snickers?"

The officer shook her head. "I'm sorry."

Maggie closed her eyes and took a deep breath. "Do you think the person who sent the flowers could have done something to him?"

"Hard to say." Officer Linton returned his notebook to his pocket. "Let us know if the cat returns."

Maggie opened the door to see the officers out and found her father poised to put the spare key in the lock. Several plastic bags were at his feet. "Dad, you have impeccable timing." She opened the door wider. "The officers are just leaving. You missed the excitement."

"Maggie, since I arrived in Somerset Harbor, I've had enough excitement to last the rest of my life." Neil hooked three plastic shopping bags on each hand and stepped into the foyer. "What's going on now?"

"I'm glad you and your fiancée are staying here, sir," Officer Crosby said. "We'll have a patrol car drive by several times during the afternoon and tonight, but it's good Mrs. Watson has someone here with her, especially at night, until we get to the bottom of this."

Maggie thanked the officers as they left, then closed the door and turned to her dad. "Daphne went upstairs to take a nap. She was pretty tired and stiff by the time my friends left."

"How are you? And why were the police here?"

"I'm tired too, but much better than this morning. Let's put the bags in the office." Maggie led the way and then pointed to a spot along the wall behind her desk. "Just set them on the floor here and I'll organize them later."

Neil followed Maggie's instructions and then stood in front of her. "You still haven't answered my second question."

"It's nothing to worry about, Dad. The police are handling it."

"Handling what, Margaret?"

She winced at the use of her full name and told him about the flower delivery and the message on the card. "The officers took the card with them. They're looking into it, so please don't let all this upset your wedding plans."

"I don't know what we're going to do with you and these mysteries you feel compelled to solve." He put his arm around her and squeezed her shoulder. "I'm going to check on Daphne now. I'll be back down shortly."

Maggie strolled into the library and sat in her favorite chair. She closed her eyes and rested her head on the chair back. Melting into the chair, she allowed her mind to drift into nothingness. Her brain was tired.

The doorbell rang and pulled her from a peaceful doze. "Now what?"

She opened the front door to find James smiling at her. "I have something you'll want to see."

"Sounds interesting." She opened the door wider. "Please come in."

"How are you feeling?" He walked in and held out a paper.

"Better. What is this?" She took it from him. It was a news story printed from the online edition of the *Somerset Harbor Herald*. Her eyes grew wide when she read the headline. She read it aloud. "'Eight Cases of Food Poisoning Traced to The Lobster Quadrille.'"

She skimmed the article. Of the eight cases reported through the hospital emergency room, three people had been admitted for extended treatment. Nausea, vomiting, fever, dizziness, headache, disorientation. It had been traced to the lobster.

"Thank goodness I don't need to add attempted murder by poisoning to the list of weird things happening to me lately." Maggie handed the paper back to James. "Though I'm not sure I can say the same for Marilyn Howland."

"What do you mean?"

"I think that Marilyn is being slowly poisoned by Forbes Easton, just enough to keep her incapacitated."

"Maggie, that's a serious accusation. People age differently.

She could be experiencing signs of Alzheimer's or Parkinson's."

"I don't have medical proof, of course, but my gut feeling is she doesn't have either of those diseases. I think someone is drugging or poisoning Marilyn. Something isn't right about that situation."

"Hmmm. It's a possibility, I suppose." James shrugged and looked to the side, then stopped and squinted at a gold metal waste can under a table. He leaned closer. "Maggie, why are there perfectly good flowers in the trash can?"

"It's a long story."

He looked at his watch. "I have all afternoon."

James listened without interruption as Maggie described the entire episode from the deliveryman on her doorstep to the police officers' arrival and report.

"Where did the flowers come from?"

"I don't know. The delivery guy didn't have a logo on his shirt, and I didn't see a delivery truck."

James reached into the trash can, pulled a piece of tissue paper away from the flowers, and held it up. "Yep, there it is."

"What?"

He handed the paper to Maggie. "Look closely and you'll see a faint design with a few waves and a mermaid tail."

"The Singing Mermaid Floral Shoppe." Maggie studied the paper. "Yes, I recognize the logo. I was so freaked out earlier that I didn't even look at the tissue paper."

"I know the owner. Think your dad might be up for a trip to the florist? Sometimes people will remember more information when a police officer isn't around." He gave her the same look parents give children before a scolding. "You can stay home and rest."

As if on cue, Neil appeared in the doorway. "Daphne's asleep. Nice to see you, James."

"Just the man I wanted to talk to." James explained his plan and the questions he wanted to ask, and Neil readily agreed. They left the house chatting like longtime buddies.

After walking them to the door, Maggie returned to her office desk and sat down. She bounced back up almost immediately. *I can't sit here and do nothing while Dad and James play detective. I must find the truth about Marilyn.*

She scribbled a note to Daphne and hung it on the refrigerator with a magnet. Maggie wanted someone to know where she was going. *Just in case.* After fetching her coat, purse, and keys, she left the house to get the answers she needed.

. . . .

"Hi, Maggie." Sue Dixon greeted her from the nurse's station outside Marilyn's room. "Are you here to read to Mrs. Howland?"

"I am." Maggie held up the book. "I keep it in my car so it's ready when I have a few spare minutes to pop in here."

"I'm so glad she has a visitor who's not her son-in-law," Sue said, frowning. "Normally it's nice when family comes, but it's creepy how often he sees her. He's here every day."

"Mr. Easton is pretty protective of his mother-in-law. He's not thrilled about my reading to her. He was quite blunt in telling me I wasn't needed."

Sue shrugged. "He'll get over it. He didn't provide a list of unwelcome visitors, so you're free to read to Mrs. Howland anytime you like."

"Thank you. I'll let you know how today goes," Maggie said, turning to Marilyn's room.

"Maggie." Sue called her name before Maggie reached Mrs. Howland's door.

"Yes?"

Sue motioned for Maggie to come closer. "I wouldn't

normally say anything like this, but since we're friends, I will. I think Mrs. Howland gets worse after her son-in-law visits."

"How so?"

"She'll be fine when she wakes up, but she becomes disoriented after he visits."

"What are you saying?"

"The longer between his visits, the better she seems."

"Are you sure her disorientation isn't dementia?"

"Privacy laws prevent me from saying any more, but I'll just say that I'm glad someone else has noticed her . . . symptoms. I don't have enough proof to go to the authorities with my suspicions."

"I see. Thank you for sharing this with me."

"You're welcome."

Maggie crossed the hallway to Marilyn's room. She pushed the door open and found the woman sitting up in bed. "Hello, Mrs. Howland. I'm Maggie. Do you remember me from my last visit? I read to you from *The Count of Monte Cristo*."

The older woman smiled. "That was you reading? I don't remember the face."

Maggie nodded. "I thought I'd read the next chapter, if you'd like."

"Please do. I enjoy company. I don't see many people." Her eyes were clearer than they had been previously, but her body seemed to waver slightly. "I'm afraid I'm sleepy again, though."

Maggie smiled kindly. "It's all right if you fall asleep. I can always come back."

Maggie pulled the chair closer to the bed, sat down, and opened the book to the marked page. She began reading and soon became engrossed in the world of Edmond Dantès as he went from carefree youth to wrongfully convicted felon. From time to time, Maggie glanced up to check on Marilyn. By the end of the chapter, the older woman's eyes were closed and her mouth was gaping. Maggie slipped in the place marker and closed the book. She studied the woman's lined face, peaceful in sleep.

"When is the last time you've checked on my mother-in-law?" Forbes Easton's voice boomed across the hallway.

Maggie froze. *What would Forbes do if he found me here against his wishes?*

Maggie's heart pounded so hard she felt it in her ears. Leaving wasn't an option. He'd see her. Where could she hide? She panned the room. Restroom? Too risky. He might need to use it. The reading chair by the window wasn't large enough for cover. She spied a door in the far corner of the room. The closet. Maggie scooped up her purse and coat in one arm and clutched the book in the other, then tiptoed across the room so her boots wouldn't make a sound or leave scuff marks on the shiny polished floor.

She slipped the book under her arm with the coat and opened the closet door as slowly as she dared in hopes Forbes wouldn't hear her. Maggie slipped inside and eased the door shut. Closing her eyes, she leaned against the side of the closet and slowly exhaled. *I made it.*

When she opened her eyes and looked around, Maggie saw she wasn't alone.

19

The man clapped a hand over Maggie's mouth before she could scream. She struggled against him, but he was too strong. He put his mouth to her ear and whispered, "Don't scream. I won't hurt you. Listen."

She tried to see his features, but he was standing beside and slightly behind her. He removed his hand from Maggie's mouth and placed a finger over his lips, signaling her to stay silent.

"My dear mother-in-law, you look as though this place is agreeing with you." Now in the room, Forbes's voice was loud and clear, dripping with venom. "I can't tell you how much I enjoy living in the mansion, but what I'm really enjoying is making it suit my tastes. It's such a relief getting rid of all that old junk. You don't mind, do you? After all, you can't possibly use it here." Maggie turned her head toward the door and realized it hadn't quite closed all the way. *Please don't walk to this side of the room.*

She needn't have worried. Forbes was enjoying the sound of his own voice too much to pay attention to his surroundings. "You know, *Mom*, I enjoy our little chats so much that I brought you another treat."

The talking stopped. Maggie held her breath. The man next to her did too. She no longer felt his breath tickling her face.

"That's a good girl. Have some more. It's your favorite, mint chocolate chip with extra green goodness. Drink up fast—it might not stay frozen long with its special ingredient."

Marilyn cleared her throat. "No. I'm not thirsty. I don't want any more." Her voice was barely audible.

"Sure you do," Forbes growled. "And you're going to drink this." Forbes began to pace around Marilyn's room. "You might as well. It'll make this place more bearable. You're certainly not coming back to the Twisdem Mansion. Or should I say, the Easton Mansion. This is your home now."

Maggie saw the light in the room shift as Forbes walked toward the closet door. The man beside her stiffened. *Lord, please keep him from opening the door.* Forbes's footfalls came closer until his shadow crossed the crack in the door. *Please keep us safe.* The closet door clicked shut and the footsteps moved away from it.

Maggie sagged with relief, and she eased her coat, purse, and book to the floor by the closet wall to relieve her tight arm muscles. With the door closed and two people breathing in tight quarters, the closet had become unbearably stuffy. What felt like an eternity passed. Maggie no longer heard talking or movement outside the closet, but she feared what would happen if she opened the door.

Her closet companion leaned forward and put his ear to the door. "I think he's gone." His voice was barely a whisper.

He turned the handle and eased the door open, then stepped halfway out into the room. After a few seconds, he motioned for her to follow him. They crept into the room. The man stopped at Marilyn's bedside and took her pulse before grabbing Maggie's hand and pulling her out of the room.

The hallway was deserted, but Maggie's eyes jumped from side to side and corner to corner looking for any sign of Forbes. She didn't get a good look at the man who held her hand until they were safely out of the building. She pulled her hand out of his and he turned to face her fully at last.

It was Fedora Man, hatless today, his long gray hair hanging loose over his shoulders. Now that she got a good look at his face, something about it seemed vaguely familiar. *Probably because I've been seeing him everywhere I go for the last several days.*

"So, besides the guy I pepper-sprayed in this parking lot, chased through a backyard, and saw at the Twisdem auction, who are you?" Maggie demanded.

"I'm Marilyn's brother. Scott."

It can't be. "Scott Twisdem died in a car wreck in 1970. Try a different lie." Not that she really wanted to hear any other lies, especially since he might have been responsible for the car accident and the other unpleasant things that had been happening. She'd rather just get out of there.

Maggie suddenly realized that she had left her coat, purse, and book inside. She shoved her freezing hands into her jeans pocket and her right hand hit metal. *I put my car keys in my pocket.* She could return for her other things later. She dashed for her car.

"Wait." The man caught up with her and grabbed her arm. "Please. I have to trust someone, and you are kind to my sister. Help me save her."

"Save her?" Maggie pulled her arm away and studied his face. His eyes were brown, like Scott Twisdem's. His height seemed about right. But it was like comparing grapes to raisins to match photos of an eighteen-year-old kid with a man in his late sixties. She'd read once that eyes are windows into the soul, so she held Fedora Man's gaze. She saw sadness and fatigue, and a love for Marilyn. "You believe she's being drugged or poisoned too?"

Rage flashed in his eyes. "I think he's trying to kill her. You heard his quip about the 'special' ingredient. I think it's antifreeze."

Maggie remembered her first visit to the nursing home. *Marilyn asked about her brother.* "When I went to visit Marilyn the first time, she asked me where you were. I wondered if she had dementia or her medication was clouding her memory." She saw concern in the man's face. "But you really were there, weren't you?"

He nodded. "I arrived right before you did. I was pretending to read a newspaper while you were talking with her."

"We can go to my house. My father, his fiancée, and my friend James will be there. I trust them, and you can too." *I hope we can trust you.*

Maggie rubbed her hands on her sweater sleeves and jumped up and down. "I ran out of Marilyn's room without my coat and purse. They must be in the closet. What are the odds Forbes is lurking around in there waiting for us?"

"About even, I guess." Scott glanced at the entrance. "Let's go back inside. I'll go to the room and get your things. He doesn't know me. You can duck into the ladies room in the lobby and wait for me. I'll tap on the door on my way outside."

Maggie didn't want to go back inside. "I can wait in my car and you can follow me to Sedgwick Manor."

"You're safer inside, Maggie."

"Wait. How do you know my name?"

Scott smiled. "You bought the one item from the mansion I really wanted. I made it my business to find out your name."

"The sideboard?"

"I'll tell you everything at your place. Right now, let me go get your stuff before my sister's son-in-law finds them and figures out you know his secret." He put a hand on her arm. "Please come inside with me. Then we can leave together."

Maggie looked over the parking lot and considered her car, sitting forlorn in a remote area. She decided to take a chance. "Okay."

. . . .

Later, Maggie walked into the formal living room at Sedgwick Manor with two cups of coffee, still trying to wrap her mind around the fact that Scott Twisdem was sitting on her sofa. "Here you go—one cup of black coffee."

She sat in the adjacent chair with her own coffee and studied the man in front of her. He'd trimmed his long beard into a mustache and goatee since she saw him at the auction. He'd put his hair into a ponytail on his way to the manor. "So, explain to me how you came back from the dead."

He stared into his cup for a minute before looking at her. "I think you already know some of it after talking with my old girlfriend and my best friend's family. And I'm sure Mr. Welborn was helpful too."

"So my imagination wasn't playing tricks on me. I really was being followed," Maggie said, a mixture of anger and relief in her words.

"I didn't understand what you were doing. I was trying to figure out how to get my old treasures back."

"I was researching the history of the family and furniture. I always write up a background story about the antiques for our customers. I know a little about you. Not—"

Voices traveled from the foyer, and a few seconds later, Daphne strolled in with Neil and James.

"Maggie, there you are." Daphne had an arm linked with each man. "Look who I found walking in the door as I came downstairs." Her hand flew to her cheek when she saw Scott sitting on the sofa. "I'm sorry, I didn't know you had company."

Neil gaped at the man talking to his daughter. "Maggie . . . what is Cole Loveren doing sitting in your living room?"

Maggie laughed to break the tension in the moment. "Dad, I think you have some wishful thinking going on. This, believe it or not, is Scott Twisdem."

"Maggie, the man sitting on your sofa is Cole Loveren. I should know—I've been his biggest fan since I was in college. How did you two meet?"

"Actually, you're both right." Scott rose to his feet. "Maggie and I met at Fair Winds Nursing Home. We were visiting my sister at the same time."

"I'm James Bennett, a friend of Maggie's." James stepped toward Scott and held out his hand. "And I think you have some explaining to do."

"And I'm anxious to hear it, but first tell me what the florist said." Maggie cut her eyes to Scott. "Please tell me if you had anything to do with the flowers I received this afternoon."

Confusion filled Scott's face. "I owe you a huge bouquet of flowers for your kindness to my sister, but I can't take credit for them."

If he loved her so much, why did he walk away from her?

"We were fortunate to find out anything at all," Neil said. "I think we would have been out of luck if James didn't know the owner."

"The shop manager said the flowers were purchased yesterday by a man in an obvious disguise," James explained. "A bad toupee, a crooked fake mustache, and a crumpled suit two sizes too large."

Maggie's father lifted his hands in frustration. "He paid cash and signed the card himself. He refused delivery."

James leaned forward in his chair. "Maggie, do you remember what the deliveryman looked like and what he was wearing?"

Maggie closed her eyes in concentration. "I was so tired from being sick all night, I didn't pay that much attention. He wore blue jeans and a denim jacket. Black cap. Couldn't see his hair for his cap."

"Short or tall?" James urged her to remember.

"I don't know. Kind of short, I guess."

James eyed Scott with suspicion. "Are you sure you don't know anything about this?"

"Not a thing, but I'm curious. What did the note say?"

Maggie didn't want to believe Scott had anything to do with the note. She preferred to think of him as the likable artistic teenager Cynthia had dated. "It said, 'Let sleeping dogs lie or you'll be sorry.'"

"Sounds like it could have been written by a rock star trying to keep his true identity secret." James's tone was assertive but not mean.

Scott closed his eyes and took a deep breath. "I've done some things I'm not proud of in Somerset Harbor, but I promise I didn't mean to hurt anyone, and I certainly didn't send the flowers."

"Mr. Loveren, or Twisdem, whatever your name is, I think you'd better explain what you just said before I call the police," James said, pulling his phone from his pocket.

Scott took a deep breath. "My promoter scheduled a concert in Portland, and I saw it as a chance for me to come back and face my past. But when I arrived in Somerset Harbor, I found auction signs posted outside the family home. I'd been gone nearly fifty years, but I was shocked to see my family's belongings up for sale. I tried to buy back as many as I could. When I discovered my sister was alive, I was over the moon. Then I found out what he'd done to her. What he's still doing to her." Scott's voice, soft and silky smooth when singing, had a gravelly edge to it as he spoke. "I had no intention of hurting or scaring anyone. I only wanted to save my sister and some family heirlooms."

The room was silent as Scott owned up to rummaging through the box of items outside Carriage House Antiques, attempting to break into the shop, and peeking in the window while Maggie was playing music.

"All of that was you?" Maggie was dumbfounded. "Can you explain how the box of records and other items ended up outside of the antiques shop?"

He nodded. "I was snooping around the outside of the mansion one day when I heard the housekeeper grumbling to the gardener. Forbes had told her to get rid of a box of items that hadn't sold at the auction, but when she saw the contents, she decided to take it to the antiques shop instead of the garbage." Scott looked each person in the eyes. "I'm truly sorry for scaring you and breaking the window. I'll pay for any damages."

Maggie studied the man who had confessed to wreaking havoc on her life over the last couple of weeks. He seemed sincere. But she wasn't completely satisfied. "What about Snickers?"

"Sorry?" Scott's eyes held question marks.

"My cat, Snickers. What did you do with him?"

Scott shook his head. "I've never seen your cat." His gaze never wavered, but his eyes softened. "I'd never hurt a cat."

"Oh." Maggie wasn't sure whether to be relieved Scott had nothing to do with the cat's disappearance or disappointed he hadn't provided a clue to Snickers's whereabouts.

"And the car wreck that sent Daphne to the hospital? That happened on our way back from your concert." Neil's voice was accusatory despite his Cole Loveren hero worship.

"I don't know about a wreck," Scott said. "I wish I had information for you."

Maggie looked away from Scott and gazed out the window to the ocean. The rising full moon cast a glow over waves breaking on the shore. The grandfather clock began chiming the six o'clock hour.

When it stopped, Daphne rose to her feet. "Maggie, it's been a long day and we have a lot to discuss here. I'm going to see what I can whip up for supper. And before you ask, I don't need any help. You guys keep sorting things out." Daphne put her hand on Scott's shoulder. "For what it's worth, I believe you." She grinned at her fiancé. "And my judgment isn't clouded by hero worship."

"Is this a private party or can anyone join?" June strolled into the living room. "I don't mean to interrupt, but I thought I'd stop in and say hi before going home."

"Your timing is perfect." Maggie motioned June into the living room. "Here's someone you need to meet."

Scott stood up as June approached the seating area.

"June McGillis, meet Scott Twisdem," Maggie announced.

"Say what?" June did a double take. "You mean the same Scott Twisdem who died nearly fifty years ago?"

"One and the same," Scott said. "People know me as Cole Loveren these days."

June stepped forward and offered a handshake but did a double take when she was close enough to get a good look at Scott's face. "You're Fedora Man!"

"Fedora Man?" Scott looked confused.

Maggie chuckled. "We called you Fedora Man when you started outbidding us at the auction."

"Ah, I let my beard grow longer than my usual goatee and mustache before my trip to Somerset Harbor. Wore my long hair under the fedora at the auction. My attempt at being incognito in my hometown."

June was still staring at the man they'd believed was dead. "All these years, you've been a local legend, forever eighteen years old in the minds of Somerset Harbor residents. But you've been a music legend for decades. How?"

"Don't answer yet." Daphne strolled into the living room wearing Aunt Evelyn's apron and waving a ladle. "Ladies and gentleman, dinner is served buffet style in the kitchen with casual seating in the breakfast room. Further questions must wait until we have food in front of us."

Despite her fiancé's grumbling about the interruption, Daphne herded them into the kitchen to serve themselves soup from a big stockpot on the stove. A stack of colorful bowls sat nearby on the counter.

"In honor of your return from the dead, why don't you start things off?" She handed the ladle to Scott.

"I don't know, I was raised to let the ladies go first," he said, offering the ladle to Maggie.

"Oh no." Maggie shook her head. "You're the guest of honor."

Scott smiled and Maggie understood why he'd become a superstar. He was a talented musician, startlingly handsome, and polite to boot—unless he was breaking and entering.

When everyone was seated around the table with a bowl of homemade vegetable beef soup and generous slices of thick brown bread, Neil looked at Scott. "So, how did Scott Twisdem become Cole Loveren?"

All eyes turned to Scott with anticipation.

He stared into his soup bowl for a while before looking at the silent faces around the table. "I've spent most of my life trying to atone for what happened on the night I killed my family and best friend. I guess it's time someone knew what happened. Maybe I can stop running from my past."

Maggie caught her breath. *He killed them?*

"High school is a tough time for any kid," Scott continued. "But it seemed like life was suffocating me. My girlfriend was talking marriage. Dad had already contacted his cronies at Harvard. He had it all planned—graduate from Harvard and get on the fast track to taking over the Twisdem empire. Uncle Sam wanted me to fight a war I wasn't sure I believed in." Scott dipped his spoon in his soup bowl and stirred, watching the steam dissipate into the air. "All I wanted to do was go to art school."

The room was silent, save for the clink of silverware against bowls, while everyone waited for Scott to continue. Maggie was about to urge him on when he laid his spoon on the table and took a deep breath.

"My saving grace had always been my buddy Will. We became friends in first grade, despite our different backgrounds. His family was comfortable but not rich. His mom had been a nurse during World War II and worked in the Somerset Harbor hospital. His dad was an accountant. Will's world was real and a welcome relief from being a Twisdem, where life revolved around European travels, country club parties, and the all-encompassing family empire."

Scott rubbed his eyes and paused before continuing. "Our friendship was strained because I was spending more time with Cynthia and less with Will. We were still friends, but he began hanging out with Philip Johns, who headed up a local garage band. Philip was a good kid, very personable and a good guitarist. Will wanted to be like him."

Maggie recalled her conversations with Cynthia and Pop. "Everything changed when Philip enlisted, didn't it?"

Scott nodded. "Especially after Philip was killed in Vietnam. Will was devastated. He went from being a gentle soul to a bitter anarchist overnight. I felt guilty about the change in our friendship, and it bothered me to see him so crazed after Philip's death. I started tagging along to his war protests, partly to assuage my guilt and partly to keep him out of trouble. I found myself pulled deeper into the volatile antiwar movement."

"That's when Cynthia returned your class ring, right?" Maggie sipped a spoonful of soup and was pleased when, after the night she'd had previously, her stomach accepted the nourishment without protest.

"Cynthia said I was more interested in the movement than I was our relationship, but she was wrong. I was trying to save my best friend from himself. Instead, I killed him."

Maggie stiffened. *He said it again.* "Scott, how did you kill Will and your family?"

Scott took a drink of water. "On the afternoon of the accident, Will showed up at the mansion as we—Mother, Father, Marilyn, and I—were leaving for Portland to attend a gallery opening my father was sponsoring. Will had quarreled with his mom and dad, who said he had a duty to serve his country."

"According to Will's brother and sister, he'd been arguing a lot with their parents about the war, college, and his music," James said.

"He was arguing with everybody at the time, even me." Scott looked at James. "Will didn't want to go to college, so he was all about dodging the draft and escaping to Canada. I knew I could avoid the draft for several years by going to school. I figured the war would have run its course by then."

"Oh!" June's outburst raised eyebrows and everyone at the table looked at her. "Maggie and I found your draft cards—yours and Will's—inside the hidden drawer of a sideboard."

Scott smiled for the first time since he began telling his story. "I was hoping to find them the night I tried to break into the antiques shop. I'd like to see them."

Maggie surveyed the half-empty soup bowls and bread plates lining the perimeter of the table. "We can go to the shop when we finish eating, if you like."

"The soup can be reheated." Neil pushed his chair from the table. "I say we take a look inside the hidden drawer now."

James raised his eyebrows. "Maggie, don't you still have the cards and the other items we showed the Rackelmans?"

Maggie shook her head. "I didn't feel right hanging onto

them, so I asked June to put everything back in the hidden drawer until we were ready to sell the sideboard."

"I stand corrected." James stood. "Let's go to the shop."

The small group dispersed to retrieve their coats and gathered at the side door to traverse the path to Carriage House Antiques. The night was cold and still, but the air crackled with excitement. Soon they'd have the answers to Maggie's questions.

Maggie escorted the group down the path and unlocked the shop door. "We set up several different vignettes with the pieces from your family," Maggie explained, leading the group to the second such display. She stopped and motioned Scott toward the sideboard. "The key is in the left drawer. I think you should open it."

Scott nodded and stared at the piece as if seeing a specter from his past. He ran his hands over the top of the sideboard, tracing the dark wood inlay. He removed the key from the left drawer and inserted it in the center lock. The group watched the rock star pull out the drawer to reach the hidden compartment behind it. He slid his hand around inside the drawer and fished out his class ring. He pushed it onto the ring finger of his right hand. "I can't believe it still fits." He lifted his hand and twisted the ring around his finger. "I never put it on again after Cynthia returned it. I always thought I'd give it back to her one day. Looking back, I'm sure my marrying her, or anyone else at that time, wasn't part of my father's plan. Harvard and the Twisdem Corporation came first."

Scott left the ring on and reached into the drawer again, this time retrieving two small, faded pieces of paper. He closed his eyes, drew a deep breath, and exhaled slowly. "Will wanted to burn his draft card the night my family was headed to Portland. He brought a lighter to the house with him."

Silence hung in the air until June broke it. "How did they get into the hidden drawer?"

"Will and I hid stuff in the drawer from the time we discovered it in sixth grade. We'd put things in there and take them out depending on what we wanted to hide from our parents. The ring went into the drawer as soon as Cynthia returned it. We put the draft cards in there while my father was warming up the car for the trip to Portland. I guess I was hoping out of sight, out of mind, and that Will would eventually give up on burning it. I told him we could burn them after the trip to Portland."

Neil leaned in to get a closer look. "What happened next?"

"Will's argument with his parents started that afternoon when he told them he wasn't going with them to visit relatives in Vermont and he wasn't going to Vietnam, either. He'd made plans to go to Canada. He told me he was putting those plans into motion now that his number had been picked in the draft lottery. He'd come to say good-bye," Scott said. "In the end, my mother talked Will into going with us to Portland, but I knew it was only delaying his inevitable hitchhike to Canada." Scott shook his head. "I should have known it'd be a disaster."

Maggie shivered. "What happened?"

"As we drove out of town, the conversation turned to the war and the future. My father began lecturing Will about patriotic duty, going to college, having a career in business." Scott shuffled the draft cards. "The more he lectured, the harder Will tried to convince him that he was wrong." He sighed. "Mom was in the front seat trying to calm my father. Marilyn was sitting on the other side of Will, attempting to distract him from the argument. I couldn't take the bickering. I finally did something I'd never thought I'd do: I raised my voice and told my father to lay off Will because not everyone was cut out to be like a Twisdem."

The air in the shop was heavy with suspense.

Scott rubbed his hands over his face and continued. "My

father was livid. He turned around, shook his fist at me, and started yelling. The rest happened so fast, it's still a jumble in my mind. He lost control of the car. We spun off the road." Scott's eyes filled with tears. "We went airborne into the ravine and crashed at the bottom."

Somewhere in the shop, a grandfather clock ticked. Outside, a neighbor's dog barked. Maggie put a hand on Scott's shoulder to provide some sort of comfort, but she didn't know what to say. The group waited for him to regain composure.

"Will was motionless beside me. Neither of my parents moved in the front seat. Marilyn had been thrown from the car." Scott's voice sounded distant, as if he were talking in his sleep. "I scrambled out of the car to find her. I couldn't believe how far away she landed. I was trying to feel for her pulse when the car burst into flames."

Maggie squeezed Scott's shoulder, tears spilling down her cheeks. "You don't have to tell us any more," she whispered.

Scott looked at her. "I do. I've made a career out of pushing my memories aside and burying them in music. It's time to face it." He wiped a hand over his face. "I climbed back to the road and tried to wrap my mind around the fact that my family and my best friend were dead. And it was my fault. I'd distracted my father and caused the crash. I killed them with my disrespect," Scott said, sounding more like a young man than a rock star in his midsixties. "Shame, fear, and grief drove me to a decision that forever changed my life."

He paused and looked at Maggie, who nodded encouragement.

He shuddered. "I made my way back into town and climbed through Will's bedroom window, like we'd always done. I picked up the stuff I'd need to start a new life: Will's duffel bag, clothes, cash from his secret hiding place, and his guitar. Since I had gotten Will killed, I felt obligated to live the life he'd always wanted. I hitchhiked to Canada, changed my name, and became Cole Loveren, rock musician."

"Holy smokes!" Neil's eyes widened. "Now I know why that poem was so familiar."

"This poem." June pulled the aged paper from the sideboard and handed it to Scott.

"It was a song on your very first album, but it never made it to the charts." Neil's expression was the same as a child's on Christmas morning.

"It is, indeed." Scott read the lyrics, mumbling the words to himself. "Will and I did have some fun back then. It wasn't all protests. He had been giving me guitar lessons, and we discovered I had a knack for it. We started writing this song together not long before the accident. We were both trying to make sense of ourselves and each other."

Maggie looked over Scott's shoulder and pointed at the red smudges on the paper. "Are those fingerprints?"

He nodded. "We made a blood vow to remain friends no matter where the war might take us. I didn't realize I'd be the one going to Canada."

"What brought you back to Somerset Harbor?" said James, a hint of suspicion still in his voice. "Was it the auction?"

"I didn't know about the auction until I showed up at the mansion and found it crawling with people. I had a concert scheduled in Portland, so I decided to arrive early and take a side trip to my hometown. I figured I wouldn't be recognized after nearly fifty years." He chuckled. "Most of the time people don't even recognize me as Cole Loveren. I fly under the radar these days."

Scott wandered from one piece of Twisdem furniture to another. "I'm glad I happened upon the auction and had the chance to buy back some pieces." His expression darkened. "They wouldn't have been up for sale in the first place if it weren't for Marilyn's loathsome excuse for a son-in-law."

"What do you mean?" June asked.

"To put it bluntly," Maggie said, "Marilyn's son-in-law is making himself comfortable in that house because he doesn't expect her to come home. We're convinced that he's poisoning or drugging her to gain control of her assets, and he's going to leave her in Fair Winds indefinitely."

Scott pulled up a chair from his childhood home and motioned everyone closer. "The question is: How are we going to stop him?"

21

When Maggie pulled into the Fair Winds parking lot the next morning, Scott was leaning against his car, sipping from a to-go cup. Dressed in blue jeans and a brown leather jacket, he seemed less menacing bathed in sunlight. "Good morning, Fedora Man," Maggie said, getting out of her car. "You forgot your hat."

"I guess I'll have to come up with an appropriate nickname for you." He grinned and took a swig from his cup. "So, our plan is to talk to the nurse about Forbes and see if Marilyn can tell us anything, but leave out the heroics, right? I promised your dad I'd keep you in line."

"Right. If we're in luck, my friend Sue Dixon will be on duty. Depending upon what the nurse says, we might need to talk with someone in administration. At the very least, we can put someone on notice to watch for a son-in-law bearing unwanted gifts." She was still trying to grasp the reality of talking with Scott Twisdem and Cole Loveren in one person. "And I can't believe Dad still thinks I need protecting."

"You're a gutsy woman, Maggie, and gutsy women have a tendency to need protection from time to time." He drained his cup and tossed it into a nearby trash can. "It's showtime. Let's go."

They signed in, the receptionist buzzed them through the inner door, and they approached the nurse's station. "We're in luck. I see Sue." Maggie gave her a wave.

Scott tugged Maggie's coat sleeve. "I want to see Marilyn before we talk to anyone else. I need to make sure she's okay."

"I understand," Maggie said.

Sue approached them. "Good morning, Maggie. You've arrived before Mr. Easton today."

"We're going to go in and see Marilyn now, and then I hope you'll have time to chat a minute."

"Sure. With any luck you can get a good visit in before Mr. Easton shows up."

Maggie thought she saw a look of disgust pass across Sue's face. "I hope so," she said as she and Scott walked away.

When they entered room 121, Marilyn was sitting up, the head of her bed raised to support her back. Scott pulled the door partially shut behind them, his eyes glued to his sister. Her eyes were alert and she smiled at her visitors. Maggie's heart swelled with joy as she watched the siblings connect.

The joy was short-lived.

"Well, good morning, Mr. Easton." Sue's voice echoed in the hallway before anyone in Marilyn's room could speak. "How are you this morning?"

"Fine, fine," Maggie heard him reply. "Just brought Mother Howland one of her favorite milkshakes."

As Sue kept making small talk in the hallway, Scott held his finger to his lips and motioned to the closet. Marilyn nodded once, her head dropping to the side and eyes closing in feigned sleep. The closet door was barely shut when Maggie heard Forbes's footsteps enter the room.

"I think you're getting too popular, mother-in-law dearest." Forbes's voice dripped with sarcasm. "That Watson woman's been on the sign-in sheet every time I've come this week. Not to mention somebody pretending to be Cole Loveren. What a laugh."

Marilyn mumbled. Maggie leaned closer to the closet door to listen.

Forbes continued his rant. "I made it very clear to her to leave you alone."

Marilyn murmured again.

"What did you say to me?" Forbes was icy and controlled.

Marilyn cleared her throat. "I said go away." Her voice was stronger.

"Me? You're telling *me* to go away?" A loud thud echoed through the room as what sounded like the milkshake struck the closet door. Maggie recoiled when the door vibrated. "I'm your family. I'm supposed to be here. But—"

The closet door flew open and Maggie found a gun with a silencer thrust in her face. Forbes's eyes were blazing, his lips contorted in a sneer. "Hello, beautiful." He held up her copy of *The Count of Monte Cristo*. "Looking for this?"

Her book. She'd forgotten to tell Scott to get it yesterday when he returned for her coat and purse.

Maggie lifted her head and swallowed her fear. "I was."

"Well, you found it. Not that you'll have a chance to read it," he said. "Get out of the closet. Now." Forbes waved the gun and positioned himself between his captives and the room's only exit. "Mind the mess. Don't want you to slip and hurt yourselves before I can finish the job." He leveled the gun at Maggie. "My plan was working until you and this long-haired hippie started hanging around the nursing home. Reading? Yeah, right. You were making trouble. Couldn't mind your own business, could you?"

Forbes's face was red, and his eyes flashed wildly. Maggie thought he looked like he was about to explode. *He must be nuts to think he could get away with shooting someone in this type of facility.*

Out of the corner of her eye, Maggie saw Marilyn push the nurse call button on her bed. *Please God, keep Forbes's eyes on me.* "I was researching the antiques I bought at your auction. That's my business." Did she dare egg him on? She had to stall for time. "You're wrong about something, though. Twisdem Mansion will never be yours. Marilyn's brother will inherit it before you will."

"Shows how much you know." Forbes waved the gun in front of her face, smiling in triumph. "Marilyn's brother has been dead for years."

Keep him talking. "I know for a fact he's alive. He may return at any moment to take what's rightfully his."

Maggie felt Scott move closer to her and grasp the back of her upper arm. *What is he doing?* She'd left the top zipper of her purse open, and his hand slipped inside. From the pressure she felt on the shoulder strap, Maggie knew he was fishing for something. She stifled a smile. He was lifting the pepper spray from her bag.

Forbes's eyes flashed as he paced back and forth between the closet and the bed. The barrel of the gun vacillated between pointing at Marilyn, then sweeping back toward Maggie and Scott. On the next pass, as Forbes glanced at Marilyn, Scott pulled the canister from Maggie's purse and tensed, ready to spring toward Forbes.

The room door flew open at the split second Forbes turned to look out the window. "Police! Drop your weapon and put your hands in the air."

Forbes thrust his hands in the air, releasing the gun, which clattered to the ground and landed in a puddle of melty green ice cream. In an instant, the room was swarming with police officers. Officer Crosby went straight to Marilyn's bedside while Officer Linton approached Maggie and Scott.

Scott slipped the pepper spray back into Maggie's purse as they watched the scene unfold. Forbes was handcuffed by Officers Samantha Clayton and Peter Williams. Maggie was glad to see them. Forbes might have been in handcuffs, but his eyes remained wild.

With Marilyn's villainous son-in-law restrained, Maggie found her voice. "It must have been you behind all of the dangerous things that have happened to me over the last week. The headless doll, the threat at the concert, and the flowers were bad enough, but running us off the road the other night?" Maggie's fear turned to anger. "You put my father's fiancée in the hospital right before her wedding day."

"What?" Confusion snapped Forbes out of his rage. Shaking his head slightly, he raised his eyebrows. "Don't be silly. What are you talking about, dolls and flowers?"

Maggie looked into his eyes. *He certainly seems surprised, even offended.* But if Forbes wasn't responsible for everything, who was? And why? The recollection of seeing Scott get in the dented SUV after she pepper-sprayed him muddied her thoughts.

"Yeah, yeah." The older officer pointed Forbes to the door. "We'll get everything sorted out at the station."

"You can't arrest me. I didn't do anything. I was only protecting my interests here." Forbes's eyes were blazing again. He pointed at Maggie. "It's all her fault. She poked her nose into my business and began asking questions about the family. You obviously don't know who you're dealing with. I'm Forbes Easton! I want my lawyer." The officers hustled Forbes into the hallway. The sound of his ranting was audible until the electronic doors in the lobby closed behind him.

Maggie watched Marilyn talk with Officer Crosby. She turned to Officer Linton. "Is she all right, Robert?"

"I think so. The doctor here will examine her to be sure."

"How did you know to come here and save the day?" Now that the fracas had ended, questions were pinging around Maggie's mind like pinballs.

"Your nurse friend called us when she thought she saw a gun in Mr. Easton's waistband. Thanks to her, he didn't have time to hurt anyone." Officer Linton looked at Scott. "Who are you?"

"I know who he is." All heads turned toward Marilyn when she piped up. "He's my brother, Scott. I'd know him anywhere, even though he's older and has gray hair." She crooked her finger at Scott. "I do think he'd look better without the facial hair, though."

"She's right on both accounts," Scott said, nodding. "I am Scott Twisdem, and my face could probably use a shave. But my legal name now is Cole Loveren."

"Yeah, right." Officer Linton rolled his eyes. "And I'm Justin Bieber."

Scott pulled his passport from his inside jacket pocket and handed it to the officer. "I changed my name when I moved to Montreal in 1970. I'm a Canadian citizen now."

Officer Linton stared at the passport. "Well, I'll be," he said to his partner. "He really is Cole Loveren." He held out the passport to Scott. "I need to ask you some questions."

Scott's eyes were fixed on his sister. "I'm happy to answer your questions, but may I speak with my sister first? We haven't had a real conversation since 1970."

The two officers nodded and Scott pulled a chair up to his sister's bedside.

"Marilyn, I'm so sorry." He wrapped his hands around Marilyn's left hand and lifted it to his chest. "You were covered in blood. Lying crumpled on the ground. My fingers were on your wrist when the car burst into flames. I didn't feel your pulse or see your breath." His tears fell onto the crisp white bedsheet.

Marilyn's eyes were fixed on Scott's face. "I tried to tell the police Will had been in the car with us, but nobody believed me." Her voice was raspy. "They said I had selective amnesia. Everyone thought I had a screw loose after the accident."

"You were never crazy." He bowed his head and sat silently for a minute. "I was dazed sitting next to you when the car blew up. I lost my family and my best friend. All I had was the Twisdem money and obligations. I didn't want them. I walked away and never looked back. But I never would have left if I'd known you were alive. I'll never forgive myself for leaving you there to die."

"Look at me, little brother." She smiled when his eyes met hers. "You were here now, right when it mattered. I forgive you. It's time to forgive yourself. Nearly fifty years is a long time to shoulder blame."

Scott nodded. "I'll work on it."

Sue Dixon cleared her throat as she entered the room with a slender, dark-haired woman in a white lab coat. "Officers, this is Dr. Sark. She's here to examine Mrs. Howland now that we know . . . what we know."

Officer Linton nodded and addressed Maggie and Scott. "I'll need you both to meet me at the police station to file a complete report." He looked at Scott. "We're going to discuss how you assumed Will Rackelman's identity."

"I never used Will's name or identification. I only took some clothes, a little cash, and his guitar." Scott's voice indicated fatigue. "Times were different then. But I'll tell you everything at the station."

Officer Crosby approached the doctor. "Dr. Sark, Mrs. Howland said her son-in-law has been bringing her these milkshakes for a while. She didn't want to drink them, but he threatened her daughter. She told me he said he added a 'special green ingredient,' and she always felt dizzy and disoriented after drinking them. Sounds to me like he was feeding her tiny doses of antifreeze, and we'll have this cup tested to be sure. For now, though, you might want to treat her accordingly."

"Certainly," Dr. Sark said, scribbling a note on the folder in her hand. "Now, if you'll all excuse me, I need to attend to Mrs. Howland."

Maggie gazed out the window at the midday sky. Her father and Daphne were probably getting worried. With the wedding only two days away, they had last-minute details to iron out. *And have they found Snickers?* She pulled her cell phone from her purse. "I need to make a quick call, and then I'll be on my way to the station." Maggie put her other hand on Marilyn's shoulder. "I hope to see you soon."

The older woman beamed at her, her eyes refreshingly sharp and alert. "Me too, Maggie."

· · · · · · · · · · · · · · · · ·

At daybreak, Maggie slipped outside to search for Snickers. After searching the manor property again, she braved the wind and headed down Shoreline Drive. She went into every open shop to ask if anyone had seen her faithful companion.

Maggie was freezing and exhausted by the time she'd walked every block in downtown. She searched every nook and cranny she could find and spoke with each person she saw. Her concern for Snickers grew. He never stayed out this long. Where could he be?

When she returned to Sedgwick Manor, she found Scott sitting on the sofa with his guitar across his lap giving a private concert for her father. Daphne, curled up in a wingback chair, studied her wedding checklist.

Daphne saw her first. "Any luck?" Genuine concern filled her eyes.

"Not a sign. I covered every foot of downtown, but nobody has seen Snickers." Maggie's voice wavered. "I'm beyond worried."

"I see I'm here at a bad time, Maggie." Scott leaned his guitar against the sofa and stood up. "I came by to ask you to visit Will's family and Cynthia Moorman with me. I'd hoped you'd be able to help soften the shock a little."

"I don't know what else I can do here except worry about Snickers. I'm happy to go with you, unless Daphne needs me for wedding errands."

"Thanks to you and your friends, we have the wedding covered. Ruth called me with an update. They'll be here at the crack of dawn tomorrow." Daphne held up her list. "Look at all those checkmarks. Go on and help Scott."

. . . .

The American flag still waved in front of Will Rackelman's home as Maggie and Scott crossed the walkway to the porch. Maggie rubbed her gloved hands together. "Remember, when I called this time, I didn't tell them why I wanted to stop by. I'm sure they'll know it has something to do with Will. Are you sure you're ready for this?"

"I have to be ready. I'm several decades late."

"Let's do it." Maggie knocked on the door.

A few moments later, Ron opened the door. "Maggie, welcome." He held out his hand to Scott. "I'm Ron."

"Scott."

"And this is my sister, Gloria." Ron waved them to the sofa. "Please, sit down."

As they had during Maggie's last visit, the siblings sat in the matching chairs. Ron stared at Scott until his eyes widened in a flash of recognition. He leaned forward. "It can't be. Cole Loveren? I went to your concert the other night."

Maggie's heart jumped. She hadn't counted on Ron recognizing Scott as his famous alter ego. Cole Loveren may have had his first hit decades ago, but people certainly remembered him.

"I am." Scott looked first at Ron and then Gloria. "But you and your brother, Will, knew me as Scott."

A deafening silence filled the air. Maggie waited for someone to speak. The next words were not hers to say. The siblings looked at Maggie with the unspoken question: *Is he telling the truth?* Maggie nodded.

"But you died in the car wreck in 1970." Gloria brushed her hair out of her face as if it would help her see the truth better. "How is this possible?"

Scott moved to the edge of the sofa and leaned forward. "I'm not the one who died in the wreck." He inhaled a breath and let it out. "Will did. I'm so sorry."

Ron sat motionless. Maggie searched for signs of emotion of any kind, but his face was unreadable. His sister vibrated with silent sobs as tears stained her face.

"But his guitar was gone, his cash stash emptied, clothes were missing." Gloria's voice was shaking.

Maggie once again listened as Scott explained Will's unannounced arrival at the mansion, described the fiery wreck, and told of his split-second decision to make a break for Canada and leave his old life in Somerset Harbor.

"I felt responsible for the deaths of my parents, my sister, and my best friend. My girl had broken up with me. The only thing I had left was Will's dream. In a moment of desperation, I chose to live it for him."

Ron shook his head, moving for the first time since learning of his brother's death. "Why didn't you tell us? Mom and Dad died believing Will took off because they were riding him so hard about his protesting."

Scott cringed at Ron's words. "I was a kid, terrified I'd be arrested for dodging the draft. By the time I was old enough to understand the consequences of what I'd done, I was surrounded by managers, handlers, security guards, music label reps. My life wasn't my own any more than when I was Scott Twisdem, but at least I was free to create art with my music. Will's music." Scott wrung his hands. "Not a day has gone by that I haven't thought of Will. Cole Loveren is a memorial to his dream. One of the songs on my first album was partially written when Will and I were hanging out in his room. After I hooked up with a manager in Toronto and began working on the album, I added a couple of verses and titled it 'Ghosts of the Past.'"

"Now I remember that song. Those were some of the lyrics you showed us, Maggie. It wasn't a poem." Ron's voice was husky with emotion. "It reminded me of Will with its alternating stanzas of rebellion, love, and regret."

"I think of him each time I sing it." Scott peered at each of Will's siblings. "I hope you can forgive me."

Ron and Gloria looked at each other hesitantly.

Scott stood up. "I have three sons from my late wife. The oldest is named William." He pulled two cards from his pocket, handing one to Ron and the other to Gloria. "I know you'll have questions. This is my private number. Only a few people have it. I hope you'll call if I can do anything for you."

Scott hugged Will's brother and sister before they could protest. "Please call me," he said. He walked to the front door and then through it with Maggie trailing behind him.

· · · · · · · · · · · · · · · · ·

"This house suits Cynthia," Scott said, pulling his rental car alongside the curb in front of the yellow-and-white Victorian. "She had a quiet, sunny personality."

"Still does." Maggie saw an excited teenage boy under the gray beard and mustache. His hair was pulled back in a ponytail. "She's had a good life. Loving marriage, two doting children, and beautiful grandkids."

"Good. She deserves it."

Maggie placed her hand on the door handle. "Are you sure you want me to go with you?"

"Yeah. She might be unnerved at the sight of a strange man at her door."

As they entered the gate, Scott's eyes cut to the trees, confirming Maggie's belief that she'd been watched by Fedora Man during her first visit to Cynthia. He was silent as they climbed the steps and rang the doorbell. Seconds ticked by and he began fidgeting with his car keys. Maggie was about to suggest that they return later when the door opened.

"Maggie, how nice to see you again." Cynthia's smile was genuine. Her gaze drifted to Scott.

"Cynthia, this is my friend Scott. Forgive our dropping by unannounced, but may we come in?"

"Of course." Cynthia opened the door and ushered them into the living room.

Maggie sat on the love seat. Scott joined her after Cynthia was seated in the chair. The older woman's gaze was fixed on Scott's face.

Scott eased to the edge of his seat. "Cynthia, it's me. *Scott.*"

Cynthia squinted her eyes and leaned forward. "Those are Scott's eyes. But how?"

Maggie listened as Scott once again told the story of the accident and the life-changing decision he made in its aftermath. Each time she heard him recount the event, Maggie felt she knew the man better.

"I don't know what to say." Cynthia's face was unreadable. "I imagine most of us would want to both hug and slap you."

Scott flinched. "I deserve that."

"Yes." Cynthia was calm and controlled. "You broke my heart twice. First by choosing Will and his protests over me, and then dying before we had a chance to try again."

"I never got you out of my head." Scott returned her gaze. "As I watched the car burn, I thought about how I'd lost my family, my best friend, and you. You'd made it clear you didn't want me. I had nothing to keep me in Somerset Harbor."

Maggie cleared her throat. "Cynthia, Scott did come by your house."

"You did?" Cynthia looked at him. "When? How did you find me?"

"At first, I was following Maggie to see what she was doing. While she was inside the house, I did an Internet search on my phone to see who owned it. I was curious why she was talking to you."

"You didn't forget me."

"Never. I came back again because I needed to see how you were doing. I wanted to know if you were happy."

"I am. My husband has been a blessing. I've had sadness, though. After forty years of marriage, my Carleton is losing his battle with Alzheimer's and it's hard on both of us. Our children help us through it, especially my son, who lives nearby."

Silence filled the room and Maggie waited for Scott or Cynthia to continue.

"I'm sorry if I scared you." Scott stared at his lap. After a long moment, he locked eyes with Cynthia. "I loved you. What happened to us, really?"

Scott listened without interrupting as Cynthia explained her aversion to the war protests.

Scott's sigh filled the room. "The protests were all about Will. He was irritated with me for spending so much time with you, so I tried to make up for it by going to protests with him. I didn't want to choose between my best friend and my girl."

Cynthia pulled a tissue from her pants pocket and dabbed her eyes. "I'm sorry too. How fortunate are we to have a chance to apologize and put the past behind us?"

"We are lucky." Scott's eyes were moist too. "I need you to know, as Cole Loveren, I wrote and performed songs about love and peace and respect for soldiers."

"Cole Loveren? The musician?" Cynthia's hands covered her mouth in surprise. "You're Cole Loveren?"

Scott spent the next half hour fielding questions about his life and career from Cynthia, the old easiness between them returning as the minutes passed. Maggie and Scott excused themselves after Maggie received her fifth text from an increasingly nervous bride. Scott promised to see Cynthia again before heading back to Canada, and Maggie invited her to visit Sedgwick Manor when the wedding festivities were over.

"How do you feel?" Maggie asked as they approached the rental car.

"Like the weight of a lifetime has been lifted from my shoulders."

She hugged him. "You did the right thing by visiting Will's family and Cynthia. All of you needed closure."

When they reached the car, Scott opened the passenger door for Maggie. She paused before climbing in and said, "I wish you could also explain the other strange things I've experienced lately."

"Me too," Scott agreed as Maggie's phone buzzed with a new text.

She pulled the phone from her purse. "It's Daphne again." Maggie read the text aloud. "'Come home *now*. Big trouble.'"

"Who are you, and what are you doing in my house?" Maggie stared at the bald man she'd seen arguing with Scott at The Busy Bean what seemed like an eternity ago. He was flanked by Officers Linton and Crosby. Her father, Daphne, and James stood clustered by the library door.

The man glared in return. His face and hands were covered in scratches. "I was returning this blasted cat of yours. Don't know why so many people like 'em anyway. This critter is downright mean."

Snickers meowed from halfway up the stairs.

"Snickers! There you are." Maggie knelt down as the cat leaped down the steps and ran into her outstretched arms.

She stood, cradling a purring Snickers in her arms, and addressed the bald man. "What were you doing with my cat? And who are you?"

"He's my road manager," Scott said, stepping into the foyer next to Maggie. "Lorne, what have you done?"

Lorne inspected a welt rising from a long scratch Snickers left on his wrist. "I didn't mean any harm. I thought if she was preoccupied with looking for her cat, then she'd stop trying to find out your identity. But she wouldn't stop."

Scott inclined his head. "And the rest of it?"

"What d'you mean, the rest of it?"

"Lorne, we go back decades. I know you. What else did you do?"

"I may have put a headless doll in her car."

"And?"

Lorne looked at the ground. "Threatened her at your concert."

A hand squeezed Maggie's shoulder and she looked up to see James staring at her with raised eyebrows. Behind him, her father had the same stern expression on his face. She should have told them about the threat before the concert started. "I didn't want to spoil the evening," she murmured to them. Both men shook their heads.

"I sent the flowers too."

Scott stepped closer to Lorne. "Lorne, tell me you didn't cause the accident. It was a pretty strange coincidence for them to be run off the road so close to where my parents died."

Lorne raised his head and returned Scott's stare. He flinched under his employer's glare. "I didn't mean to hurt anyone. I just wanted to keep you from connecting with your old life in Somerset Harbor. I thought it would lure you into retirement. I was trying to protect you, like always."

Officer Crosby scribbled notes in her pad. Her partner's fingers were resting on the handcuffs clipped to his belt.

Scott shook his head in disbelief. "We've been friends for forty-five years. You've done a great job of protecting me. But this goes beyond protection. How did you always know where to find Maggie?"

"You'd be surprised what you overhear in a small-town coffee shop." He glowered at Scott. "I wouldn't have done any of it if you'd listened to me when I called you during the auction. I knew it wasn't a good idea for you to go nosing around in your past. That's why I told you the press was at the mansion and they might snoop around enough to recognize you. But you couldn't leave the past alone. You had to go looking for trouble."

Scott's eyes showed the pain of betrayal. "You hurt innocent people and tried to keep me from making peace with my past. Unbelievable."

"Yeah, well, who saved your bacon when this goody-two-shoes pepper-sprayed you in a parking lot? She's lucky you didn't want to press charges."

"Who could blame her? I scared her. Lorne, how could you?"

"My top priority has always been your career, Cole."

Everyone watched as Officer Linton handcuffed Lorne and read his rights.

Officer Crosby smiled at the bride and groom, then Maggie. "Now that we have accounted for everything, have a beautiful wedding."

Maggie linked arms with her father and Daphne. "We will."

The officers escorted Lorne to the door.

"I'd better follow them to the station. Lorne is my responsibility." Scott shook his head. "I'm sorry I brought all this unpleasantness to your life."

"We're all fine." Maggie placed her hand on his forearm and squeezed. "Go do what you need to do."

Maggie walked him to the door and stood on the threshold watching Scott follow his road manager and police escort to the cruiser. Lorne might have acted out of fierce loyalty and fear of losing his job, but damage had been done. She didn't envy Scott for the tough decisions he was facing regarding his friend.

"Maggie? How are you doing?" James asked.

"I'm all right. Relieved it's over." She smiled at him. "I'm glad you were here."

"Me too. I'd stopped by the coffee shop and Daisy asked me if I had time to bring a few serving dishes over here so she didn't have to load them up tomorrow morning. I was in the kitchen when Lorne rang the doorbell and Daphne answered it. He was shouting, so I called the police before I came to the foyer to distract him."

"Alderman Bennett saved the day," Daphne said, giving him a one-armed hug. "A good man is a blessing to have around."

. . . .

"You are stunning," Maggie said as Daphne imitated a model's pose in the center of Emily's bedroom. Her soon-to-be stepmother was glowing like a young bride. "My friends are downstairs putting the finishing touches on the flowers. The foyer, living room, and dining room are fit for Hollywood royalty. I've never seen Sedgwick Manor look so gorgeous."

Maggie smiled at the last secret she held. *I can't wait until she walks into the living room and sees her kids and Dad's siblings.* The family from Michigan had arrived early that morning, and Maggie had kept them hidden in her sitting room.

Daphne reached her hands out to Maggie and pulled her into a hug. "Thank you for welcoming me into your home and family." Daphne stepped back and looked at Maggie. "I know everything happened so suddenly. Meeting me and planning a wedding in a week must have been overwhelming, yet you've been so gracious."

"It's been a whirlwind, that's for sure." Maggie looked at the pink scar where Daphne's stitches had been. Many women would have made a fuss about it, but Daphne was unfazed. She was beautiful despite the reminder of the crash. "After everything we've been through, I feel like I've known you a long time."

Daphne reached up to check the small spray of roses and lily of the valley tucked in her hair over one ear. "I feel the same way, which is why I asked you to stand up with me. It means the world, really."

"I'm honored to stand beside you during the wedding. You put life back into my father's eyes. I never thought I'd see him so happy again." Maggie glanced at the bedside clock. "I'd better check on things downstairs. Do you need me to do anything?"

"I'm finer than corn silk at harvesttime. Don't worry about me."

Maggie giggled. "Somehow I think you can handle anything coming down the pike. I'll let you know when we're about to start."

She closed the door to Emily's room and walked to the guest suite, where she tapped on the door. "Dad? Need anything?"

"Not a thing, Mags. I'll be down in a minute."

"We're doing great on time, Dad. Head to the living room when you're ready."

Maggie headed down the stairs. The front door opened as she reached the bottom step. "Mom, I'm home," Emily called as she walked into the foyer.

"I'm so glad you're here. Just in time." Maggie embraced her daughter.

"Mom, you look amazing. You should wear dusty rose more often." Emily eyed the staircase, decorated in flowers and ivy. "When did you have time to decorate?"

"I didn't. Thank God for good friends. Ruth and Fran did the flowers and decorations. Daisy took care of the food. Ina and Liz helped Daphne find her wedding dress."

The doorbell rang and Maggie opened the door to find Scott with a guitar in one hand and his sister smiling by his side. "Good morning. I'm thrilled you could join us." She stepped back and waved them inside. "Emily, would you please take Mrs. Howland and her brother to the living room? We're almost ready to start."

Maggie took a quick pass through the dining room, where Ruth and Fran were putting the finishing touches on the table decorations. The table was set with china and silver dating back to some of the earliest Sedgwicks. A bed of greenery, pink roses, and lily of the valley connected two ornate silver candlesticks. "The dining room is stunning. I know it wasn't easy keeping Daphne away until now, but she'll be overwhelmed when she sees it."

Ruth and Fran stepped back from the table and looked at their handiwork. "Everything's ready here," Ruth pronounced.

"Good." Maggie grinned. "I think it's showtime."

Maggie peeked in the kitchen and waved to get Daisy's attention. "Smells fabulous. We're about to start the ceremony, so head to the living room when you can."

By the time Maggie made it to the living room herself, Scott was quietly strumming his guitar. Ruth and Marilyn sat on the sofa talking softly while Fran, Ina, and Liz sat in the small grouping of chairs behind them. Emily and Pastor Young stood near the fireplace going over the Bible passage she was to read during the ceremony.

Maggie approached Neil and James, who were standing by the window, watching the sea and chatting. "I think we're about set. Are you, Dad?"

Her father hugged her. "Ready, willing, and able." He kissed the top of her head. "Thank you for giving Daphne the wedding she's always wanted. You've been a trooper."

"More than anything in the world, I want you to be happy." Maggie's gaze traveled over the people in the room—family, friends, and new acquaintances who were already tied to her in a way she couldn't describe. "Loved ones mean everything in life."

She kissed Neil's cheek and waved to Pastor Young as Daisy entered the room and sat in an empty chair. "Here we go."

Maggie went to her sitting room and led the visitors from Michigan into the living room. Her father grinned when he saw them and flashed a thumbs-up sign.

The talking ceased and Scott began playing a song he'd written for a friend's wedding decades ago. Maggie climbed the stairs to lead her father's bride to him.

"All set?" Maggie asked, poking her head into the room where Daphne waited. She plucked the bride's bouquet from the dresser and handed it to her.

Daphne flashed a radiant smile. "More than you know."

Maggie picked up her smaller bouquet in one hand and held the other out to Daphne. "Let's get to it."

The two women walked to the door. Maggie said, "When I get to the third step, start your descent, okay?"

Daphne nodded and blinked back tears. "I'm not going to cry."

"You're allowed to cry at your wedding. You'll still be beautiful." Maggie started down the steps. *This place was made for weddings.*

Neil, now with his brothers beside him, waited in front of the window overlooking the sea. Maggie's heart swelled as she entered the room and saw the smiles on her friends' and loved ones' faces. She took her place as Daphne's attendant and grinned when her new stepmother walked down the aisle and saw not only her groom but her children too. Tears of joy streamed down Maggie's cheeks as her father pledged to honor and cherish this woman who had given him a second chance at love.

The crowd tittered when Daphne, in heels, bent down to kiss her new husband in response to Pastor Young saying, "You may now kiss your bride."

Neil chuckled with them and tilted his head up so his lips could meet hers.

After the group's applause subsided, Scott launched into "I Only Have Eyes for You," and the groom took his bride into his arms. Maggie stood transfixed, watching them sway and gaze into each other's eyes.

When the song ended, Scott placed his guitar to the side and stood up. "Congratulations to the happy couple," he said. "Thanks for including me. I brought all sorts of trouble to your lives, and I don't know how to make it up to you."

Daphne hugged the musician with enthusiasm. "Trust me, playing at our wedding more than makes up for it. You've been Neil's favorite singer since he was in college. Having you here was the perfect gift."

The reception passed in a blur of toasts, family stories, laughter, cake cutting, and good wishes. Maggie reveled in spending time with her Michigan aunt and uncles. Before she knew it, her father had luggage piled by the door and the rental car parked out front. Although the number of single women in the room was small, Daphne insisted on throwing her bouquet to the few widows and unmarried ladies. She climbed halfway up the staircase, turned so her back was facing the crowd, and tossed her bouquet right into Maggie's hands.

Everyone erupted into cheers and laughter. Emily nudged Maggie with her elbow. "Gee, Mom, you could have at least given me a chance." The laughter continued.

"I-I'm—" she stammered, heat spreading across her face. James stared at her, grinning.

"Mom, you're blushing." Emily beamed.

Maggie fought to regain composure. "Well, it isn't every day a woman my age catches a bridal bouquet, but I guess the odds were in my favor in this group."

Daphne approached and threw her arms around Maggie's neck. "Maggie, I've loved getting to know you. Keep an eye on James because he's a good one, and you deserve a gentleman."

"James is wonderful, but I'm doing fine on my own."

"Oh, shush." Daphne made goo-goo eyes at her new husband. "Maybe *he* needs *you*."

The historical society ladies gave their best wishes to the couple and retreated to the dining room and kitchen for cleanup. Daisy paused outside the dining room and turned to Maggie. "Don't you even think about stepping foot back here. No KP duty for you. Just relax for a change."

Maggie was familiar with the determined look on Daisy's face. She had to admit her energy was fading fast. "Will do. Thank you."

"I'm proud of you, honey." Daisy backed into the dining room and closed the door.

After Emily said good-bye to her grandfather and new grandmother and went to the dining room to help, Maggie lingered in the foyer.

Daphne took Maggie's hands in hers. "Thank you for opening your home and heart to me. Our wedding was just as beautiful as Sylvia Sterling's, thanks to you and your friends."

"My home is your home. You and Dad are always welcome here." Maggie squeezed Daphne's hand. "Seeing the look on Dad's face when he said 'I do' was incredible. I love seeing him so happy."

"My turn." Maggie's father wrapped her in a hug. "Let's be better about visiting each other. Deal?"

"Deal," Maggie replied.

"Come visit in the summer. The farm is beautiful and the weather mild." Daphne winked. "Bring Emily with you. I promise to spoil you rotten."

Snickers meowed and made figure eights around Maggie's ankles. She picked him up and held him close as her father and Daphne grabbed their suitcases and walked to the car. "Do you know how much I missed you, Snickers? Any chance I can turn you back into an indoor kitty?"

He answered with a meow and struggled in her arms. "You may as well stay still. I'm not letting you out of my sight for a long time."

They stood in the doorway and watched the sedan disappear down the street, knowing her father wouldn't vanish from her life again. His heart had finally healed.

When Maggie backed into the foyer and closed the door, Scott, Marilyn, and June were waiting for her.

Scott held out a check. "I'd like to buy back the pieces you bought at the auction. I trust this will cover it. If not, let me know." He handed the check to Maggie, who nodded and passed it to June. "I'm sorry I was so forceful in trying to get them from you in the beginning. I was shocked to return and find my childhood home being dismantled. I'm afraid my judgment was clouded."

"No harm done," June said. "Stop by the shop when you have time and we can go over the pieces I have left and arrange for their delivery back to the mansion." She held up the check. "I'll take this to the shop now and come back to help with cleanup."

After June left, Maggie smiled at the siblings. "I'm happy to know you're both still alive and you've reconnected. I'm sorry Blair will have to deal with Forbes, but at least she has her mother home with her now and an uncle in her life."

"I promise you, Twisdem Mansion will remain in the family," Scott said, putting an arm around his sister. "Marilyn will retain ownership, and I'll be a frequent visitor."

"I'm glad to hear it." Maggie bent down and released a squirming Snickers.

Marilyn's lip quivered. "Maggie, I don't know how to thank you for bringing my brother back to me."

"He was already on his way back to you once he discovered you were alive. We may have complicated each other's lives for a while, but in the process, I believe we became friends."

"You and Scott saved me from Forbes, and I'll always be grateful." The older woman hesitated. "Maggie, my friends fell away from me after he put me in Fair Winds. Even in my drugged state, I enjoyed your visits. I thought maybe we could read books and meet to discuss them once a month or so."

"An excellent idea. We can start now." Maggie linked one arm with each sibling and led them across the foyer. "Let's hunt up our first book in the library, shall we?"

Maggie paused at the library door and looked back at Snickers, who watched her from the foyer. "Well, come on. You like sitting by the fire."

Snickers stretched, twitched his ears, and scurried forward to lead the trio into the library. Everyone was home where they belonged.

Up to this point, we've been doing all the writing. Now it's *your* turn!

Tell us what you think about this book, the characters, the bad guy, or anything else you'd like to share with us about this series. We can't wait to hear from *you*!

Log on to give us your feedback at:
https://www.surveymonkey.com/r/AntiqueShop

Annie's FICTION